WHO STOLE
GRANDMA'S
MILLION-DOLLAR
PUMPKIN PIE?

THE CHICKADEE COURT MYSTERIES

WHO STOLE GRANDMA'S MILLION-DOLLAR PUMPKIN PIE?

MARTHA FREEMAN

CHICKADEE COURT MYSTERY #4

Holiday House/New York

www.holidayhouse.com
Library of Congress Cataloging-in-Publication Data
Freeman, Martha, 1956-
Who stole Grandma's million-dollar pumpkin pie? / by Martha Freeman. — 1st ed.
p. cm.
Summary: When the recipe for his grandmother's famous pumpkin pie
is suddenly missing just before Thanksgiving Day, Alex and his friend
Yasmeen try to solve the mystery of its disappearance.
ISBN 978-0-8234-2215-9 (hardcover)
[1. Pies—Fiction.   2. Thanksgiving Day—Fiction.   3. Mystery and detective stories.]
I. Title.
PZ7.F87496Wi 2009
[Fic]—dc22
2008048486

For Robert Decker,
who made a video
of me making
a pie.

WHO STOLE GRANDMA'S MILLION-DOLLAR PUMPKIN PIE?

Chapter One

When I told Yasmeen who was coming to the party, she totally dropped the football. "Zooey Bonjour, the famous TV chef, is coming to your mom's birthday party?" she said.

I said, "Yasmeen—get the ball! It's rolling away!"

Yasmeen ignored me. We have lived next door to each other since we were babies, and in all that time, almost twelve years, Yasmeen has gotten really good at ignoring me.

The ball was picking up speed on its way down the slope, so I ran around her to get it. Jogging back, I said, "Zooey Bonjour's coming with my grandma. They're friends, and they work together."

"I can't believe you never told me that!"

I shrugged. "What's the big deal?" Then I held up the ball. "Can you catch it this time, do you think?"

Yasmeen said, "I always catch it!" Then she raised her hands, ready for another perfect spiral pass thrown by future quarterback Alex Parakeet—in other words, me.

It was a cloudy Saturday morning in November. There was no wind, and the air felt like it wanted to snow but couldn't quite get cold enough. Neither of us was going to a tailgate party, so to psyche ourselves up for the football game against Minnesota, we were playing catch at Mailbox Park. Later, we'd watch the game on TV. Yasmeen and I live in College Springs, Pennsylvania, and the college team, the Knightly Tigers, is undefeated this year. The town is usually football crazy. This year it's football *nuts*.

I rocked back, cocked my arm, and threw. Yasmeen ran, reached, and caught the ball, then turned and hollered, "Go long!"

I took off, looking over my shoulder for Yasmeen's throw, which seemed to float right into my hands. I'm pretty sure Yasmeen would make a better quarterback than me, but I would never tell her that. She already thinks she's smarter and faster than me. If she finds out she's a better quarterback, she might get egotistical.

Instead of jogging back down the field, I held the ball in front of me, dropped it, and punted. Usually, I am a decent kicker, but this time the football caught the side of my foot and went off to the right. *Oops*. Yasmeen started to wave and yell, and I realized the football was about to bean an old guy in an overcoat walking innocently down the sidewalk.

Luckily, the old guy heard Yasmeen, and even more luckily, he had great hands. He didn't get clobbered the way I expected. He turned and caught the ball like a pro.

I trotted toward him saying, "Sorry."

He tossed the ball back. "Nice kick, son. But straighten it out next time, okay?"

I was going to say, "Yes, sir," but behind me I heard Yasmeen gasp. When I looked up at the man's face, I saw why. The old guy in the overcoat was totally the most famous person in College Springs: Jack Patronelli, Knightly Tigers head coach for, like, about a century.

I said the first stupid thing that came into my head. "Aren't you supposed to be at the stadium?"

"On my way," he said. "Had to go visit my new grandson on Robin Road. A little walk's good for me."

"Yes, sir," I said.

"Good luck today, coach," Yasmeen said.

"Thanks, miss." He nodded and waved. "I'll carry that with me."

"Wow," she said when he was out of earshot. "I never saw him before, did you?"

"I watch the coaches' show Tuesdays on TV," I said. "But never in person."

"My dad told me he keeps to himself," Yasmeen said. "He can't even go to the supermarket without somebody suggesting a play."

We threw the ball a couple more times. Then Yasmeen announced she had to go. She was supposed to take her gloomy genius little brother, Jeremiah, to the library, and she wanted to be back in time for the kickoff.

Walking home, I noticed every house we passed had a flag in the yard with the Knightly Tiger mascot—a tiger dressed in knight's armor—or else a tiger tail hanging from a tree branch. Yasmeen and I talked about the game, and then we talked about the birthday party for my mom that was happening after.

"With Thanksgiving coming up next week, Dad didn't want to do anything fancy," I said. "So it's just spaghetti for the food part, then the regular family birthday cake."

Then she asked a bunch of questions about Zooey Bonjour, and I tried to answer.

No, I had never met her before.

No, I had never seen her show.

And yes, my grandmother had known her for a long time—like, years, but I didn't know how many.

"Why's she coming here, anyway?" Yasmeen asked. By now, we were at the corner of our street, Chickadee Court—the same corner where, since September, the bus picks us up at 7:46 to take us to Groundhog Middle School. It's also the corner where Bub lives. He's an old guy who makes good soup and bad coffee for anybody who stops by, and he's Yasmeen's and my friend.

"It's that pumpkin pie," I said. "You know, the one my dad made last year?"

Yasmeen grinned. "Everybody knows about that— Grandma's million-dollar pumpkin pie!"

Yasmeen was probably right. Last year there was a charity auction at our old elementary school, and my dad donated this pumpkin pie made from an old family recipe. What makes the pie special is that it's made from cooked fresh pumpkin instead of canned, plus it has a secret ingredient. In fact, the ingredient is so secret it's written in code on the recipe.

Anyway, my dad's pie turned out beautiful; even my mom said so. And when people saw it and found out the story, they all wanted to bid! The pie sold for $150, the most money ever paid for a pumpkin pie in College Springs, Pennsylvania. As a joke, Bub called it "Grandma's million-dollar pumpkin pie," and the name kind of stuck.

"Did you ever find out what the secret ingredient is?" Yasmeen asked.

I shook my head. "But Dad's going to make it again this week. He's hoping we'll bring back some pumpkins from Aaron Farm when we go out there to volunteer on Monday."

"And is your grandma staying for Thanksgiving?" Yasmeen asked.

"Yeah—it's gonna be a big crowd. Besides your family, there'll be Uncle Scott and Aunt Kate, Bub, Officer Krichels, and I think Zooey Bonjour, too. Hey, do you want to stop at Bub's? Maybe he made minestrone."

"I don't have time," Yasmeen said. "But finish telling why Zooey Bonjour's here."

"She's going to broadcast her show from the tailgate before the game against Ohio next week," I said. "The way Dad explained it, her show features regional cooking, and pumpkin pie fits fall and it fits Pennsylvania. So next week, Dad's making the pie on her show."

Yasmeen stopped in her tracks. "*Alex Parakeet!* Your dad, my neighbor, is going to be on *Zooey Bonjour?* And you didn't tell me?"

"Well, sheesh, you don't have to yell about it," I said. "It's only a cooking show. Who watches them?"

I have known Yasmeen so long, sometimes I can see the wheels of her brain spinning behind her eyeballs. This was one of those times. "You know," she said slowly, "my mom's got that great peanut butter cookie recipe—the one Jeremiah likes? I think I'll make a batch for the party tonight. If Zooey Bonjour likes them, maybe I'll get the chance to be on TV, too!"

Chapter Two

My friend Bub lives in a house that's smaller than the others on our block and older. It used to be kind of sad-looking—the yard all messy and the paint peeling. But last summer, Bub started jogging with his friend, Officer Fred Krichels of the College Springs Police Department. He says since the jogging made his belly shrink, it's easier to get up and do chores. Now Bub's house has new paint, the yard's raked, and the windows are clean. A couple of weeks ago, I saw Bub outside digging, and he confessed he was planting tulip bulbs.

Today Bub heard me on his porch before I had a chance to ring the bell. "Come in!" he hollered.

I walked into the living room, stomach growling in anticipation. "Minestrone?" I said hopefully.

Bub was stretched out in the recliner watching an old black-and-white movie on TV. In his lap was Luau, my big, orange, handsome cat. Luau visits Bub all the time to watch movies. His favorites are the ones with cat food commercials.

Bub put the sound on mute and looked up. "Good day to you, too, Mr. Parakeet," he said.

"Oh, sorry," I said. "Hello, Mr. Wisniewski. Did you happen to make your world-famous minestrone today?"

Bub looked sorrowful. "I guess you'd be disappointed if I said the soup was miso."

"The one with soybean stuff?"

"Or," he said, "how about mushroom?"

"Better than miso."

"And I don't believe," Bub went on, "that you're a fan of split-pea. What if today's soup was split-pea?"

I folded my arms across my belly. "Bub, are you teasing me?" I asked. "Because I am a growing boy, and I've been playing football, and I am hungry, and I would really like to know what kind of soup you made today."

"Minestrone!" Bub said, and then he laughed his belly laugh, which is loud even now that his belly's not so big—not to mention it created a lap-quake that made my dozing cat jump.

"Mrrrow!" Luau complained.

Bub apologized to Luau, and I headed for the kitchen. Bub keeps the soup in a big black pot on the stove. It was colorful, hot, and delicious-smelling. I ladled some into a bowl, and went back into the living room. Now Luau was lying across the back of the recliner, swishing his tail, clawing the fabric, and glaring at the world. Sometimes I can understand Luau's language when nobody else can. But today anybody could have translated. My big, orange, handsome cat was *mad*.

I sat down at Bub's table, which is between the kitchen and the recliner, and spread out a paper towel to do double duty as place mat and napkin.

"Are you coming to Mom's party tonight?" I asked.

"Wouldn't miss it," Bub said. "Anybody interesting on the guest list? Besides the always-interesting neighbors, I mean?"

"Family," I said. "My aunt and uncle from Philadelphia, plus—"

"The rich aunt and uncle?" Bub interrupted.

"Right," I said. "Scott and Kate, the ones who started that website about the *Mayflower* and people's ancestors. They're here at the football game today, and they're staying through so Aunt Kate can speak at my school on Monday, and Thursday they can have Thanksgiving with us. Mrs. Aaron's coming—you know, from Aaron Farm, where Yasmeen and I volunteer? Plus there's my grandma, and this friend of hers, Zooey Bonjour."

Bub sat up straight. "*The* Zooey Bonjour?"

I looked at him. "You've heard of her, too? I don't get it. Why would anyone want to watch cooking on TV?"

Bub shrugged. "Food without the calories."

"What's wrong with calories?" I noticed that my bowl was empty. "Can I have seconds?"

"Be my guest," Bub said.

When I came back to the table, Bub was twiddling his thumbs—a sure sign he's thinking. "Which one o' my recipes do you like the best, Alex?" he asked after a minute.

"This one. Why?"

"I was thinking maybe Zooey Bonjour might want to invite *me* to be on her show. I could show the audience how I make my soup. Or—here's an idea—maybe I could reveal the secret to my aged-to-perfection coffee!"

"Go with the soup," I said.

"I think I might bring some of my soup to the party tonight for Ms. Bonjour to sample," he said, still twiddling. "Oh—and I've got a birthday present for your mom, too."

"The invitation said no gifts," I reminded him.

"Well, I can't keep it for myself," Bub said. "My ears aren't pierced. Hey—" He looked at his watch. "It's almost time to turn on ESPN. You don't mind, do you, Mr. Kitty?"

Luau said, *Mrrf,* jumped down to the floor, and swished his tail. This was slightly more difficult to translate, but I've had lots of practice. It meant: *First, you rudely awaken me. Then you try to subject me to* football! *Take me home, Alex. It's been an exhausting morning.*

I shook my head. "Luau, all you've done all morning is nap and watch TV!"

Luau looked up and blinked a long blink. *True, but my dreams were very strenuous.*

Chapter Three

The first thing I noticed when I walked into my house was a whir of the mixer from the kitchen. The next thing was the smell of chocolate. As an experienced detective, I had no trouble interpreting the clues: The whir was Dad making frosting; the smell was Mom's birthday cake, just out of the oven.

I set Luau down in the front hall, gave him an under-the-chin tickle, stood up, and shook out my shoulders. Luau is one heavy cat.

With the mixer going, there was a slight chance I could squeeze in a game of Lousy Luigi III before Dad realized I was home and started assigning chores. I was on my way to the family room when the mixer shut off and Dad called, "Alex?"

Shoot. Luau must have gone to the kitchen to check out the action in his food bowl, alerting Dad that I was home. I sighed and went to face slavery.

Dad was standing at the counter beside the sink, with the mixer and his green recipe binder in front of him. He wasted no time. "First chore," he announced.

"First lunch?" I replied.

Sure, there was all that minestrone. But soup is more like a highly nutritious snack.

"Suit yourself," Dad said. He picked up a spoon from the kitchen counter, stuck it into the bowl, and scooped out a delicious-looking blob.

I grabbed for the spoon. "*Wait!* I might like this chore! What do I have to do, exactly?"

Dad said, "Taste-test the frosting," and popped the spoon into his mouth. "*Mmm—yummy!*"

"I'm not sure your tongue is smart enough for that chore, Dad. Remember the time you forgot to add vanilla? I think I better help out." I reached to stick my finger in the bowl, but Dad batted my hand away and passed me a clean spoon. I took a generous taste and went straight to frosting heaven—smooth, just the right amount chocolatey, and plenty sweet, too.

I wanted more!

"The sugar part might not be right," I lied. "I better take another sample."

"Your 'sample' would be the rest of the bowl," Dad said. "How 'bout a peanut butter sandwich?"

I went ahead and made two sandwiches, then I got baby carrots and ranch dressing from the fridge and went to the cupboard for chips. I didn't see the usual kind, but I did see a whole bunch of identical blue and orange bags with pictures of fish on them. The label said "Cheesy Deans."

"What are these?" I asked.

"Zooey Bonjour sent them over for the party. Cheesy Deans is the new sponsor for her TV show. Go ahead and give 'em a try."

I ripped open a bag and right away was half knocked down by a sharp smell. It was sort of like cheese, but there was something else, too— like a tuna sandwich left in a backpack for a week.

Way over by the sink, Dad wrinkled his nose. "Potent, aren't they?" he said. "What do they look like?"

"Goldfish crackers—only bigger, flatter, and bluer." I reached in to give one a try, but before I could bring it to my mouth, Luau sprinted in like a lion chasing a zebra.

"Mrrrow!" he cried, which meant, *What is that* wonderful *smell? Gimme, gimme, gimme, gimme,* gimme!

I love my cat, but if he wanted one of these fish-shaped crackers, maybe I didn't?

Dad took the bag from me, read the ingredients, and laughed. "The 'dean' part is for 'sardine,'" he said. "That's the flavoring—sardine and cheese."

"Sardine, the little fish? Who would want to make a snack out of that?" I asked.

"Sardines are full of good fats, protein, and vitamin D," Dad said. "Luau seems to like the idea."

My cat was on his hind legs with his paws pressed against my knees. He was staring like a hungry orphan in an old movie: *I'll do anything, Alex. I'll clean my own litter box. Just* please *let me have one of those.*

I dropped a cracker into his bowl, and he scarfed it. Meanwhile, Dad bit off a tail fin—then squinted, bobbed his head, swallowed hard, and coughed. "Not too bad," he said finally. "But I don't want another one."

I didn't want any at all. I put the bag back and then ate my lunch while Dad loaded the dishwasher and rinsed out the mixing bowls. I told him about my morning, including Jack Patronelli, and I told him how Yasmeen and Bub got so excited over Zooey Bonjour.

All the time I was talking, Dad was working. It used to be he was not what you'd call my most energetic parent, but since he's gotten into the cooking thing, he's changed. Now, in party-prep mode, he was hyper—talking, washing, drying, wiping—all at the same time. Dad in motion equaled risky situation, and sure enough, as he was lifting the big mixer, he bumped the green recipe binder and knocked it to the floor—detonating an explosion of old family recipes.

Maybe you have noticed that sometimes parents act like kids, in which case kids have to act like parents. That's what happened now. Dad looked pretty much defeated by the sight of the recipes scattered all over the floor.

"I'll deal with it, Dad." I put my plate on the counter, then stooped down and started collecting the pages.

I guess my family is kind of unusual. It's my mom who has a regular job and my dad who mostly stays home and cleans and cooks and fixes things and does laundry. When I was little, it was different. Back then, Dad worked for an Internet company he had started with his sister, my aunt Kate. He worked all the time, but the company didn't do so well, and in the end my dad didn't have a job anymore.

It was only about a year ago that Dad got into serious cooking, but he had started to collecting recipes around the same time he lost his Internet job. Most of the recipes are old ones from his family, but he's added his own, too—recipes he finds on the Internet or in the newspaper.

Grabbing the recipes off the floor, I noticed some were smudged with food stains and coffee drops, some were handwritten on index cards that had been taped to notebook pages, and some had been printed out on scratch paper with writing on the back. It looked like a mess, but it was actually kind of an organized mess. The pages were filed by section—*Entrées, Side Dishes, Soups, Sweets*—and then alphabetically under each section. I knew Dad wanted it put back the same way, so I was extra-careful.

"Does the chocolate birthday cake go under *C* for 'cake' or *B* for 'birthday'?" I asked.

"*C*," Dad said.

"So Thanksgiving pie goes under *P*." I knew that one was extra-important, so I double-checked to make sure I was putting the recipe in its proper place under *Sweets*—right between cherry-chocolate mousse and pitty-pink pudding.

Pitty-pink pudding? I asked Dad what that was.

"One of your great-grandma Bea's recipes," he answered.

"Was she the crazy grandma?"

Dad had been chopping garlic, and now he used the knife to shove the pieces into a pan of hot olive oil. Instantly, the house smelled like a pizza. "Not exactly crazy. But she did have the idea she was such a great cook that everybody wanted to steal her recipes," he said. "That's why sometimes she wrote down ingredients in code."

I read the ingredients for the pudding. Sure enough, one of them was "4 cups fresh or frozen pitty-pinks."

"What's a pitty-pink?" I asked.

Dad frowned. "Can't remember. I know I've made it before, but I've made so many of her recipes, I get 'em mixed up. What's in it besides pitty-pinks?"

"Just sugar, cornstarch, and water," I said. "Oh, and

after pitty-pinks, it says, in parentheses, 'one word, eleven letters.' "

Dad smiled. "Right. Your great-grandma was a fan of crossword puzzles. A lot of her codes sound like crossword clues. *Hmm,* one word, eleven letters . . ." He counted off on his fingers, then smiled. "Got it. But now *you* have to guess. Think of something that's pink. And think of another word for 'pitty' or—here's a hint— 'pit.' "

"I hate puzzles," I said. "They're like homework in disguise."

Dad laughed. "I bet Yasmeen could figure it out."

Was he saying that Yasmeen is smarter than me? I mean, of *course* Yasmeen is smarter than me. But my own dad isn't supposed to say so!

I thought about it. "Cherries have pits, but that's not enough letters." I closed my eyes, and it came to me. "Raspberries! They've covered with seeds, and 'pit' is another word for seeds."

Dad smiled. "You must be my kid," he said, "because you are so darn smart."

There were only a few more sheets of paper on the floor. The last recipe was for sweet-and-sour shrimp, which I don't like but Luau loves. I set it in place, pinched the binder rings, and closed the cover.

When I stood up, I saw the clock. "Hey, it's 1:28!"

Dad clicked the radio on. "Go on in and watch," he said. "But I'm going to need some help decorating before Mom gets home."

Usually, if my mom is gone on a Saturday, it means she's working. How she says it is "fighting crime and finding bicycles." But today, for her birthday, she had a gift certificate for this place where they fix your hair and your eyebrows, and then they rub cream into you. Mom said it's the same as when my friend Ari takes his family's cocker spaniel to the groomer, only more expensive. She left early this morning—before I was even out of bed—and I was secretly afraid that when she came home, she might not look like Mom anymore.

The football game started out exciting and stayed exciting. The Knightly Tigers ran back the opening kickoff for a touchdown, and when Minnesota got the ball, we held them to a field goal. On our next possession, we drove down to the Minnesota 25, then fumbled, and Minnesota recovered. Four plays later, their quarterback completed a pass from our 18, and they had a touchdown of their own. The scoring went back and forth like that all the way to halftime, when it was Minnesota 24, Knightly Tigers 21.

"Time to decorate!" Dad hollered.

In the living room, Dad showed me how to twist

crepe paper. Luau thought the paper was a species of exotic snake, and to show it who was boss, he kept attacking the loose ends. Finally, Dad tossed him a roll all his own, and he stalked it and killed it like the mighty hunter he is.

By the time the second half started, Luau was king of the forest, and Dad had hung crepe paper all around the entire living room.

"Here's your next assignment." Dad handed me a bag of balloons to blow up. "And when the game's over, we'll tack them up in the living room, too."

Minnesota scored another field goal in the third quarter, and their defense totally shut down the Tiger offense. Twice, the cameras cut to Coach Jack Patronelli on the sidelines, wearing his orange tiger blazer, pacing up and down the way he does.

"Alex?" Dad called. "Are you blowing up balloons?"

No, I wasn't, but yes, I was planning to. "Right, Dad!"

At the start of the second half, the score was Minnesota 27, Tigers 21, and it stayed that way through the third quarter and most of the fourth. At last, with only forty seconds left in the game, we had third down and goal on the 8-yard line. If we scored the touchdown, we would tie the game, and the extra point would win it. But the Minnesota defense was tough.

I could hear Dad in the kitchen. *"Pass, Jack!"* he hollered at the radio.

That must have been what Minnesota was expecting, too, because the defensive line blitzed Corey Brown, our quarterback. Too bad for them. He had already handed off, and the running back ran around the defenders, found a hole, rushed forward, and then leaped, trying to push the ball over the goal line. *Had he made it?* Dad came running in from the kitchen to watch as the officials sorted out the bodies and finally got down to where the ball was.

"No!" we both yelled when the officials ruled the ball was an inch on the wrong side of the goal line.

There was still one down to go. If we made the touchdown and time ran out, we would still be allowed to attempt the extra point. Since this was the most exciting moment in the entire game, the TV network paused for a super-long commercial break, and between Dad and me we blew up ten more balloons. Finally, the game came back on.

"What's Jack gonna do, Dad?" I asked.

"Brown will keep it and run straight up the middle."

The teams lined up. The center hiked the ball. But Brown didn't keep it. He made a lateral to the halfback, who danced around one tackle—and across the goal line. Touchdown!

"Jack's a genius!" Dad said. "Of course, if it hadn't worked, I'd be saying he's senile."

This time there was no commercial break. Kicker Kevin Barr came onto the field, and the teams lined up. Everybody in the stadium was on their feet.

"The kick is up, a-a-a-and . . . it's *good!*" the announcer said.

The camera showed Jack Patronelli still scowling but pumping his fists in the air. I could see his breath in little puffs. Dad and I whooped, then—hollering "We won! We won!"—ran out into the front yard so we could listen to the roar of the crowd from the stadium, which was only a mile away. While we were standing in the cold, Mom's car rounded the corner, came down the street, and turned into the driveway. Dad and I waved, then linked arms and did a victory dance.

Mom got out of the car looking puzzled. "Are you celebrating my birthday without me?"

"The Knightly Tigers won!" I said.

Dad, still victory-dancing, grabbed her around the waist and gave her a big kiss, which ordinarily I would find gross.

My mom doesn't care about football, but she said she was glad everyone would be in a good mood for the party. I studied her for a second. When Ari's dog goes to the groomer, she comes home wearing a little bow.

I didn't totally expect a bow, but . . . "Mom," I said, "how come you don't look any different?"

Dad took her hand. "No nail polish?"

Mom looked embarrassed. "It seemed like such a waste of time," she said. "I was thinking I'll re-gift the certificate to Marjie Lee. She could use a break from those little ones."

"So, in that case," Dad asked, "where have you been all day?"

Mom looked at her shoes.

"*Mom!*" I said. "Did you go to the office on your birthday?"

Dad cocked his head. "Noreen . . . ?"

Mom looked up and shrugged. "It was great, actually. I got caught up on all my reports."

Dad and I looked at each other and shook our heads. Mom had always worked hard, but lately she worked all the time. Yasmeen told me there's something called a "workaholic," which means you can't stop working the way some people can't stop drinking alcohol. Was my own mom a workaholic?

Chapter Four

The people who live on Chickadee Court have a lot of parties, so by now, it's kind of predictable how the parties will go. Like, Mr. Stone will always be the first to arrive and the first to leave, and the Blancos will always be really late because they have to close up their store and Marjie Lee will always call because she has forgotten what day and what time.

The invitation to my mom's party said 7:00, and the doorbell rang at 6:59.

"That'll be Mr. Stone," Dad called from the kitchen. "Can you get it, Alex? I'm up to my eyeballs in spaghetti sauce."

I started saying, "Hi, Mr. Stone," before I even had the door open, so you can figure I was pretty surprised when the person at the door was totally not Mr. Stone. Instead, it was a tall lady with perfect silver hair, perfect eyebrows, and perfect lipstick. I had never before in my life seen anybody who looked like this.

"I'm Zooey Bonjour," the lady said in a perfectly pleasant voice. "You must be Alex. I don't believe we've met, but I've heard so much about you from Catherine."

Catherine is my grandma. I was too in awe to work my vocal chords, but luckily Mr. Stone was coming up the walk, and he rescued me.

"Good evening, Alex," he said, instead of just "hi" like usual. Then he nodded at Zooey Bonjour. "And you must be Ms. Bonjour. It's a pleasure. You know, I never miss your show."

Zooey Bonjour smiled and held out her hand, and I thought Mr. Stone would shake it, but instead he did something I couldn't believe. He raised her hand to his mouth and kissed it!

Anyone not perfect would have said, *"Eww!"* but Zooey Bonjour smiled and replied, "The pleasure is mine"—like getting your hand kissed is the most normal thing ever.

I was so surprised, I just stood there, and then my dad came up behind me. "Ted! Zooey! Nice to see you both! Alex—it's cold out here."

"You can come in," I said, which sounded dumb, so I added, "I mean, *please.* It would be so *great* if you came in."

The two of them came inside and started shedding their coats. Zooey had a flat blue purse-thing, almost like a briefcase, that she gave to Dad. Mr. Stone had to struggle with his coat because he was holding a thermos.

"I can take that for you," I said.

"Actually, it's a little something for you, Ms. Bonjour," Mr. Stone said. "I hope you won't think me presumptuous, but I've been told I make pretty good hot chocolate. I thought maybe you'd enjoy a cup yourself."

"Why, aren't you thoughtful." Zooey Bonjour looked at the thermos but didn't take it. "I'm sure it's divine. Is there a spot, Dan, where we could set it aside for later— when my palate has been properly cleansed?"

Mr. Stone didn't look so happy about giving the thermos to Dad, but finally he did, and Dad took it back to the kitchen.

The doorbell rang again, and at the same instant Byron Sikora barged in, almost knocking me over. "Where is she?" he wanted to know. "The famous TV lady? Is she here yet?" He spotted Zooey. "Are you her?"

Byron is seven.

"Why, yes, I believe I am," Zooey Bonjour said. "And whom do I have the honor of addressing?"

Sofie Sikora was right behind her little brother. Their parents were nowhere in sight.

"Ignore him," Sofie said. "He thinks you're like some ninja super-hero because you're on TV."

Byron eyed Zooey Bonjour up and down. "What's

your weapon?" he asked. "Do you have X-ray vision? Can you see my underwear?"

Sofie kicked her brother—who didn't flinch, just stuck his tongue out—and at the same time thrust a wax-paper-covered plate in Zooey Bonjour's direction. "I brought you these. They're the kind with coconut that you don't have to bake, which is good in case, like, the electricity goes out."

."Coconut tastes like string," Byron said.

"Ignore him," Sofie Sikora said.

"Hello, Sofie. Hello, Byron." My mom was coming down the stairs. She looked pretty. "Nice to see you, Zooey. It's been a long time."

"Noreen! Happy birthday!" Zooey Bonjour said. "I brought a little something . . ." She held up a wrapped present. "Shall I put it here on the table?"

Mom said, "Oh, aren't you sweet?" and I wondered what it was about Zooey Bonjour that made everybody act so formal all of a sudden. Not to mention everybody was giving her food.

My mom opened her mouth to say something else, but Sofie didn't like being ignored. "*I'm* Sofie Sikora," she said, "in case you didn't know. Alex and I solve mysteries together—along with this other girl. I'll take the paper off the cookies, and you can try one right now, okay? Have you got any milk, Mrs. Parakeet? Otherwise, they kind of get stuck on the way down. And then if you like them, Zooey Bonjour, I can be on TV showing how to make them. Being on TV will look good on my college applications, Mom says—even if it is only a cooking show on cable. Oh, I wouldn't eat the one in the corner there. That's the one Byron licked."

The cookies looked like shrunken, dried-up bird's nests. If someone had offered me one, I would have gagged, but Zooey Bonjour smiled perfectly and said, "I'm sure the cookies are delightful, dear, but I'd hate to spoil my appetite. Uh...could someone...?" She looked around.

"I'll put them in the kitchen, Zooey," Dad said, "with your purse and Mr. Stone's cocoa."

When the doorbell rang again, it was Mrs. Aaron. She's an old friend of my mom's family, and her farm out on the highway past Saucersburg is where Yasmeen and I volunteer once a week. Sometimes she rides a motorcycle, but she must have brought her truck this time. She was wearing a skirt instead of her usual over-alls. She had a shopping bag with her, and in it was a pumpkin for my dad along with a jar of Aaron Farm apricot-okra chutney for Zooey Bonjour.

Soon the house was full of neighbors eating spaghetti and salad from paper plates. Zooey Bonjour had gone into the living room, and almost everybody had followed her there to ask questions about food and being on TV and exactly what kinds of recipes she wanted on future shows because, amazingly, almost everybody had brought a sample of this or that delicious cookie-cheesecake-nacho-casserole-pie-dip for her to try when she got a chance!

About the only people who weren't in the living room were the kids. Toby Lee and Byron were chasing each other around the house, and Jeremiah, Yasmeen's little brother, sat on the stairs like a spectator at a NASCAR race, only instead of cheering, he every once in a while shook his head and said, "Uh, oh."

I listened to Zooey Bonjour for a while, but I wasn't that interested in her story about pigs finding mushrooms in the forest, so I went into the kitchen and filled my plate with more spaghetti and salad. Billy Jensen was there. He's seven, and his parents live in the nicest house on the street. He was hooked up to his iPod like always and didn't hear me when I said hi.

In the den, I found my grandma along with Michael Jensen, who's in ninth grade and too cool for kids. He was sitting on the arm of my dad's recliner and playing with his DS game. He answered my hi with a nod and a grunt, and I went over to sit by my grandma.

"Did you see the mountain of food people brought for Zooey?" I asked her.

Grandma smiled and said, "It happens all the time. People will do anything to be on TV."

"So why's Dad so lucky?" I asked. "Is it because you're his mom?"

Grandma held up her hands. "Not me," she said. "In fact, Zooey's been a little secretive about the selection process this time. All I know is she received a fan letter from someone who had tried your father's pumpkin pie and loved it. Whoever the fan was, that's who recommended the pie for the show."

"How long have you been working with her again?" I asked.

"On and off ever since . . . well, ever since she resurrected her career," Grandma said.

"What do you mean 'resurrected'?" I asked.

Grandma said, "Long story. She sort of fell out of favor for a while and didn't have a show of her own."

I was curious about what had happened, but I could tell Grandma didn't want to talk about it, so I asked about Grandma's job instead. I knew she was called a producer, but I didn't know exactly what that meant.

"It means I manage the business parts of the show, everything except the creative and the technical," she explained.

I thought about my mom—the workaholic. "When Dad was little, did you have a job?" I asked.

Grandma sipped her wine. "I didn't go to work till after your grandpa died. Zooey actually helped me find my first job, but we've been friends for years—ever since grade school over in Clear Meadow."

Yasmeen came in with her plate of spaghetti and salad. She and my grandma did their hello-hello, nice-to-see-yous, while I concentrated on slurping spaghetti without making noise. I wasn't really listening to their conversation till I heard Yasmeen say, "the million-dollar pumpkin pie."

"I didn't even get any!" she went on. "And I love pumpkin pie."

"I didn't get a piece, either," I said. "And he can only make it in the fall, because that's when there are fresh pumpkins."

"Who was it who bought the pie last year, Alex?" Yasmeen asked.

"Some name I didn't recognize."

"You know, Mrs. Parakeet, I make these really great peanut butter—" Yasmeen started to say, but right then a blond tornado blew in: *"There you are!"* And the next second, the whirlwind engulfed us, hugging and kissing and shouting about how great we all looked, and wasn't it fabulous about the Tigers beating Minnesota today? Michael Jensen took one look and retreated to the kitchen.

"Hi, Aunt Kate." I scrunched down into the sofa.

"Hello, darling." Grandma scrunched down, too.

My aunt Kate is tall, skinny, blond, and pretty. She never stops talking, smiling, or moving. Kisses over with, she dropped between Grandma and me on the sofa, put an arm around each of us, and squeezed. "Oh, it's just so *great* to be here with family and friends all together!" she said. "I'm only sorry we're late, Mom. This time of year is just so busy for the website. We're swamped, and the server went down, and Scott had to do some troubleshooting. But no way was he going to miss the game today. You know how he is!"

"How who is?" Uncle Scott appeared in the doorway. "Hey, champ!" he greeted me, "and mother-in-law, how you doin'? And"—he looked at Yasmeen—"you are . . . ?"

"Scott, you're met Yasmeen at least a hundred times!" Aunt Kate said.

Uncle Scott nedded. "Yasmeen—*right!*" he said. "Too many beautiful women in this neighborhood. How am I supposed to keep them all straight?"

My uncle Scott is such a big guy, he makes normal-sized people look like toddlers. He played linebacker for the Knightly Tigers when he was in college, and now he's a huge fan. (Get it?) He and Aunt Kate live in Philadelphia, but they have a condo here in College

Springs. They pretty much only stay in it when they come for football games.

"Are you and Zooey bunking with us tonight, Mom?" Aunt Kate asked. "There's plenty of space."

"Not this time," Grandma said. "We're sharing a suite at the Knightly Tiger Inn. Since it's business, the EAT network is picking up the tab."

"Swanky!" Aunt Kate said. "I hear they remodeled and put in big TVs—must've cost a bundle. Gosh, I'm hungry!" She bounced up. "I'm gonna get some spaghetti and say hi to Zooey. See you in a bit!"

When Aunt Kate was gone, Grandma closed her eyes. *"Phew,"* she said. "It's a good thing she has a business to run or she'd drive us all crazy." She looked at me. "I only wish your dad would find a career that he loved as much."

"He loves cooking," I said.

Grandma nodded thoughtfully. "You know, I think he just might have found his métier in food."

Yasmeen said, " 'Métier' means—"

I said, "I *know* what 'métier' means," even though I had no clue. "And I'm sure my dad has found it in food. I mean, Grandma ought to know. She's his mother."

"Speaking of food . . ." Yasmeen wrinkled her nose. "Do you smell something, uh . . . *funny?*"

"Now that you mention it. . . ." My grandmother frowned. "Isn't there a sort of nautical aroma?"

Luau must have smelled it, too. He had been dozing on the bookcase, but now he woke up and raised his head with a jerk: *Yummy!* An instant later, he was galloping toward the kitchen.

"Cheesy Deans!" I said. "Come on!"

In the kitchen, Michael Jensen, eyes glued to his DS game, was leaning against the counter by the back door. Jeremiah, Mr. Stone, and Zooey Bonjour— who had escaped from her fan club in the living room—were standing by the table. Just as I suspected, besides the spaghetti, salad, and birthday cake, there was now a bowl of Cheesy Deans.

Mr. Stone smiled at me. "I finally prevailed upon Ms. Bonjour to try my hot chocolate."

Zooey tilted her mug to show it was empty. "Divine!" she said. "And now won't you try some Cheesy Deans?" she asked him. "They're my new sponsor."

Jeremiah pinched his nose. "They smell terrible!"

Zooey Bonjour ignored him, Grandma giggled, and Yasmeen told him to shush. Mr. Stone smiled bravely, took a blue cracker from the bowl, nibbled at it, and swallowed. His Adam's apple bobbed in his throat. *"Mmm,"* he said politely.

Zooey Bonjour sighed. "People don't always take to them."

But cats do! By now, I had spotted Luau, crouched in

a shadow, with every feline system on red alert. Tail swishing, whiskers twitching, eyes flashing—he was readying himself for the attack. The only thing standing between that bowl of crackers and annihilation was me.

"Luau!" I took two quick steps, but before I could intercept him, the mighty hunter rocketed toward the table, his body making a perfect orange arc in midair.

Did I say perfect? Not quite. Luau must have been startled when I yelled, because he miscalculated, overshot the Cheesy Deans, and landed feet-first in the spaghetti. Red sauce spattered Zooey and Mr. Stone, who yelped and jumped backward, while Luau gurgled a strangled *mrrrow* that meant, *I'm drowning!* Before I could throw a life preserver, he struggled to the surface and in three fast moves jumped to the counter, dropped to the floor, and fled—humiliated—down the basement stairs.

In his wake, he left a trail of spaghetti sauce, two broken wineglasses, and Dad's recipe binder on the floor.

There was a moment of silence. Then Michael Jensen looked up and said, "Did something just happen?" which made the rest of us crack up.

"What about the cake?" Mr. Stone asked.

There were now two neat kitty paw prints in the frosting, along with one sad spaghetti noodle.

Zooey Bonjour didn't hesitate. With a perfect pink fingernail she removed the noodle. Then, using the handle of a plastic fork, she repaired the frosting.

I hadn't been totally sure about Zooey Bonjour. Wasn't she a little *too* perfect? But now I made up my mind. She was my kind of celebrity chef.

Only Jeremiah was frowning. "Don't paw prints have germs?"

Uncle Scott came into the kitchen from the hallway just then. He was carrying his plate, looking for seconds. "Something sure smells good," he said. "Hey, what are these?" He tossed back a big handful of Cheesy Deans. "Dee-licious!"

Mr. Stone and I looked at each other. Zooey said, "To some people, they're catnip."

Like he was trying to prove her point, Michael Jensen sniffed. "Smells good. Can I have some?"

On my fingers, I counted the syllables: six. That was the most I had heard from Michael Jensen in, like, a year. Uncle Scott offered the bowl to him, and he took a handful. Zooey herself took one and nibbled it daintily.

"Time for cake!" Dad's voice rang out from the living room, and the next minute I heard the mass of party guests shuffling toward us.

"Quick!" Grandma grabbed a broom and swept up the broken wineglasses. Yasmeen put the pot of spaghetti in the sink. I wiped sauce and noodles off the table.

Dad and Mom came in ahead of everybody else, just as Uncle Scott grabbed the recipe binder from the floor. By then, the kitchen was presentable—except for a trail of sauce leading to the basement stairs and the red sauce speckles on Mr. Stone and Zooey.

My dad recycles everything, and now, from a plastic baggie, he removed a handful of stubby used birthday candles, which he stuck in the cake and lit in a hurry. "Okay, gang—if we sing fast, we'll be able to get one more birthday out of these. Happy birthday to you!" he began, and everyone else chimed in.

Mom turned pink and made *tsk*ing sounds, but she was grinning. On the long, final "you-u-u!" she blew out every candle with a single big gust. Then Mrs. Aaron shouted, "Make a speech, Noreen!"

"Yes, speech!" "Speech!" other people said.

My dad likes to give speeches; my mom, not so much. She was on the spot, though, and dutifully opened her mouth to try . . . but was immediately interrupted by *Pow! Pow! Pow!* from the living room. The sound woke up Baby Alex Lee, who had been asleep in her mother Marjie's arms. Baby Alex yelled, "*Waaaaah!*" and at the same time, Mrs. Lee looked around and said, "Toby—where's Toby?"

Chapter Five

Some of the party guests ducked and squealed when they heard that *Pow! Pow! Pow!* But Bub went to investigate. It wasn't long before he returned holding a squirming, kicking Toby Lee at arm's length in front of him.

"This character," he announced, "was standing on the back of the sofa, yanking balloons off the ceiling and popping them with a thumbtack." He looked at Mrs. Lee. "You want him?"

"If no one else does," she said. "Come on, Toby. Time to get home and get to bed."

But anyone could have told her that wasn't happening. Toby wanted birthday cake, and he wanted it *now*.

Mom served him first to keep him quiet. Then she had to serve all the other little kids because they complained she wasn't being *fair*.

Zooey Bonjour was one of the last grown-ups to be served. Before she could even take a bite, Mrs. Jensen shoved a plate under her nose. "Don't spoil your appetite with *that*." She smiled sweetly. "Wouldn't you like to try one of my potato doughnuts? They're fried in lard."

Mrs. Jensen's doughnuts had been on the counter by the microwave. Now Mrs. D'Agostino grabbed the dish that she had brought. "Those old doughnuts aren't nearly as good as my crab dip." She was holding a bowl of pink glop. "If you'll wait, I'll find you a Triscuit."

By now, Mr. Blanco had a dish of white cubes in his hand. "My wife and I make this tofu ourselves," he said.

"Do you like okra?" asked Mrs. Aaron, and—like a mom feeding a reluctant baby—she held a teaspoon of lumpy-looking brown stuff to Zooey's lips.

I don't know about you, but if a whole bunch of people pushed food into my face, I'd probably push back. Like I said, though, Zooey Bonjour is perfect, and what she did was smile serenely, and address everybody at the same time: "How kind of you all to share your recipes. But as I'm sure you understand, it would be impossible to give each dish its due tonight. So may I ask a favor? Would you each just write me a brief note describing your specialty and include contact information? If we're interested, my staff will get back to you."

There was a pause; then Mrs. Sikora said, "Noreen, can I have a pen?" and soon everybody was clamoring.

Luckily, Grandma was ready for this. "We've got it

covered, Noreen," she said, and she held up a handful of pens and a pad of paper.

It was pretty soon after that that I finally got my piece of cake, which was so delicious that Zooey Bonjour herself asked to see the recipe. Dad had to look around for the old green binder, but finally Uncle Scott said, "I've got it. Gimme just another second here."

Zooey smiled. "Take your time. I'm sure it's a source of much culinary wisdom!"

"Lemme see that after you," Beth Ryan said. "Maybe there's some secret that'll tell *me* how to get picked to be on a cooking show."

"I'd like to take a look," Mrs. Jensen said.

"Then me!" added Mrs. Aaron.

By the time the binder had been passed around, it was getting late. As the guests left, they all said happy birthday to Mom—and most of them had a few words for Zooey Bonjour, too.

I was pooped, but there was still the cleanup. Luckily, Uncle Scott and Aunt Kate stayed, and so did Grandma, Zooey Bonjour, Bub, and Yasmeen's mom, Mrs. Popp. With so many people, it didn't take long.

Aunt Kate was buttoning her coat when Uncle Scott asked, "Where's the recycling go?" He was holding a stack of newspapers.

"Basement stairs," I told him.

The house was almost back to normal when Mom pointed at the pile of food the neighbors had brought. "What are we going to do about all that?" she asked.

Zooey had an answer ready. "Is anyone going to church in the morning? Some churches have potlucks after the service."

Mrs. Popp smiled and said, "Bingo."

At last, everyone was gone, and the house seemed quiet. Dad did a final walk-through in case a kid had hidden his salad under a sofa pillow. He found me zoned out in front of football highlights in the family room, and said, "Go to bed!"

"Too tired," I said.

"I'd give you a piggyback ride, but you're a little too—"

I think he was going to say "big," but I don't know for sure because right then there was a scream from right over our heads. *Mom?*

Chapter Six

Dad and I raced up the stairs and found Mom standing in their bedroom looking down at the bed. Her back was to us. She wasn't screaming anymore, but her shoulders rose and fell like she might be sobbing. In a flash, Dad had his arms around her. "Noreen? What—?"

"Mom?"

She turned halfway, and I realized she wasn't crying. She was laughing.

"I'm sorry I scared you. I was just so startled!" She shook her head. "That cat of yours, Alex. Take a look at the birthday gift he left on my pillow!"

I did, and—*Eww!*—saw the bloody remains of a big silver lizard, the kind that lives in our front yard, the kind that Luau finds so tasty.

"It's the thought that counts?" I said.

Dad laughed. "At least Luau remembered a birthday present. With the party, I almost forgot!" He opened the door to his closet, knelt down, and pulled out a big wrapped box. Then he turned to me. "I think there were a few presents left on the hall table. Why don't you run downstairs and get them?"

Bub's present turned out to be earrings that kind of looked like mini versions of the scales in the vegetable section at the grocery store. Dad explained that scales like that are a symbol for justice—a good gift for a police officer. Zooey Bonjour gave Mom a book on making perfect desserts. Grandma's gift was a card with a check in it.

"How much?" I asked.

"None of your beeswax," Mom said. The way she smiled, though, I think it was a lot.

Dad's gift, wrapped in recycled Sunday funnies, was a new silver coffeemaker, which Mom said she *loved*, even though I couldn't see how anybody could get excited over a coffeemaker. And didn't we already have one?

I thought that was it for presents, but then Mom looked over and said, "What are you giving me, Alex?"

Uh oh.

"A hug and a kiss?" I tried.

Mom nodded. "A hug and a kiss—check. *And* you can return Luau's gift outside where it came from, then bring me a new pillowcase. They're in the linen closet."

The next day was Sunday, and my plan was the same as it always is. Waste every possible minute on worthless

43

video games and mindless TV. It was about noon, and I was making solid progress when Dad called from the kitchen. "Alex?"

I couldn't answer right away. My Luigi guy was attempting a dangerous leap from one slice of pizza to another while twisting in midair and dicing a swarm of black olives with a kitchen cleaver. Executing this maneuver took both thumbs, my right pinky finger, and all my concentration.

"Alex?" Now Dad was standing in the doorway to the family room, and his voice was so loud it startled me.

"What?" I didn't look up. Luigi had escaped the oncoming olives, but a vat of tomato sauce threatened to drown him.

"Put it on pause or I'll unplug it!" Dad said.

That got my attention. "Can I help you, Dad?"

"When you put the recipe binder back together yesterday, my Thanksgiving pie recipe was in it, right?" he asked.

"I think so," I said. "Wait—Yeah, I'm sure so. I put it under *Sweets* and then under *P* for 'pie.'"

"Well, it's not there now," Dad said. "I went through every page and then turned the binder upside down. I even lay down on the floor and looked under the stove."

I glanced back at the frozen image on the screen.

If Luigi could yank the potholder out from under the vat of tomato sauce, it might tip over onto the evil—

"*Alex!*"

"Sorry, Dad. Did you say something?"

"I need that recipe so I can finish making the practice pie. With all the Thanksgiving cooking to do, I don't have much time. You know I've never been on TV before, and actually . . . I'm kind of nervous."

"You'll do great, Dad. And anyway, don't you remember what's in the recipe?"

"I've already got the pumpkin from Mrs. Aaron in the oven," Dad said, "but I don't remember proportions, and then there's the secret ingredient. . . . Will you come and look?"

I started to argue, but then I saw how worried he was. "Okay."

Like Dad, I paged through the binder. I remembered the recipes for cherry-chocolate mousse and pitty-pink pudding, which were right where they were supposed to be. Only Thanksgiving pie was missing.

"Any luck?" Dad was shaking out his other cookbooks in case the recipe had migrated.

"It's almost like somebody stole it," I said.

The timer on the oven dinged. Dad opened the oven door and pulled out the pan with the pumpkin in it. It had been round and orange when Mrs. Aaron brought it over yesterday, but now it was ugly brown and collapsing. It smelled good, though—a cross between burning leaves and maple syrup.

I asked Dad how you transformed baked pumpkin into pie, and he explained that when it cooled off, he would cut it in two, throw the seeds and the skin into the compost, mash the rest, then mix it with eggs, milk, sugar, and spices to make the custard filling.

"So you still won't reveal the secret ingredient?" I asked.

"I would," Dad said, "except for one very good reason."

"What's that?"

"I can't remember it."

I could not believe this. "But, Dad, you still know Pittsburgh Pirates' batting averages from when you were ten! How can you have forgotten an ingredient in a recipe you made last year?"

Dad shrugged. "Your great-grandma outsmarted me. She had so many good recipes and so many secrets—after a while, I couldn't keep them all straight."

"Do you remember the clue, at least?"

Dad closed his eyes and frowned. "I remember it said 'two words,'" he said, finally, "but other than that, nothing." He sighed. "I guess I'll have to tell Zooey to find somebody else to be on the show. She's certainly got plenty of volunteers."

Dad was trying to act like he didn't care about being on TV, but I knew he did. And even though I didn't want to admit it, I had a feeling there actually was something I could do to help him out.

I think I mentioned before that Yasmeen and I— along with Bub and Luau and even that annoying loud-mouth Sofie Sikora—have solved some neighborhood mysteries.

The thing is, though, that every time I start detecting, I promise myself I am not going to do it again. It is really hard and not necessarily fun. One time, we even had to sort through bags of month-old, smelly trash. Besides that, detecting can get dangerous. We've confronted ghosts, kidnappers, thieves, and some extremely creepy cats. No way did I want to put myself through all that again. I was plenty busy with homework, video games, and football in the park.

"You okay, Alex?" Dad put his hand on my shoulder. "Looks like you've got a headache."

I told Dad I was fine. Then I said, "This is sort of like a mystery, isn't it? So maybe . . ." I hesitated. "Maybe I should call Yasmeen."

Dad smiled. "I was hoping you'd say that."

Chapter Seven

Yasmeen's attitude about mysteries is a little different from mine. What I mean is, she loves them.

When I called her up, her family had just gotten home from church. I explained what had happened. While I talked, I was standing in our family room, looking out the front window.

"Be right there," Yasmeen said.

I put the receiver down and started counting off the seconds. Before I even reached "five one-thousand," I saw a shape streaking across our yard, and at "seven one-thousand" the doorbell rang.

I opened the door. "I think that was a new record," I said.

Yasmeen pushed past me, headed for the kitchen. "You were wearing gloves when you looked at the recipe binder, weren't you?"

"Uh . . . not exactly," I said.

"Oh, Alex!" she said. "Aren't you ever going to learn?"

"It wasn't a mystery when I looked through the

binder," I said. "It was just a lost recipe. It only became a mystery when I called you."

"Hi, Mr. Parakeet." Yasmeen walked into the kitchen. "I understand you need the services of the Chickadee Court Detective Agency."

Dad was rolling out pie dough. "Only if you're offering low, low prices to friends and neighbors."

"I think we can work out easy payments," Yasmeen said. "I'll take a piece of your million-dollar pumpkin pie—just as soon as we get your recipe back."

"It's a deal," Dad said. "Meanwhile, I'm going to experiment with recipes. Maybe I'll get lucky and stumble on the secret."

Yasmeen wanted to take a look at the binder. I told her that Dad and I already had, but like I said, Yasmeen is good at ignoring me. Together we sat down at the kitchen table, and she flipped through the pages till she'd examined every one. Then she looked up and announced, "The pumpkin pie recipe is not here."

I folded my arms across my chest. "Now I know why everybody says you're so smart."

She ignored me again. "I think we should start with what Bub always says: means, motive, opportunity. Figure that out, and we've figured out the thief."

"But who says there even *is* a thief?" I asked.

"Be logical, bud. You're sure the recipe was here

yesterday, and recipes don't walk away. Now, *means* is first. In other words, who had the ability to steal the recipe?"

I shrugged. "Anybody with fingers to open the binder rings, which probably lets out Luau. Only . . . well, I guess it would have to be somebody who could hide the recipe somewhere to get it out of the house, somebody with a bag or something."

"So more likely a lady than a man," Yasmeen said, "because ladies have purses."

"Unless whoever stole it didn't take it away," I said.

"But why would anybody steal it if they didn't take it away?" Yasmeen asked.

"Why would anybody steal it in the first place?" I asked

"That's not means, that's *motive*," Yasmeen said.

"Fine—we'll do motive. Somebody would steal the pie recipe because . . ." I looked at her, hoping she would fill in the blank.

Yasmeen thought for a second, and then she frowned. "I can only think of one reason," she said. "And that's because the person doesn't want your dad to make the pie—like maybe somebody doesn't want him to be on TV."

"But everybody likes my dad!" I protested.

"That's not the point," she said. "Look how everybody acted last night at the party—crazy to give Zooey

Bonjour a cooking sample so they could get on TV. If Mr. Parakeet was out of the way, it might make a spot for somebody else."

I understood what Yasmeen was saying, but I didn't like it. Who would be mean enough to steal my dad's chance? So I changed the subject. "Let's do *opportunity*," I said. "Who not only could have taken the recipe but had the chance to take it? We know it disappeared sometime between when I put it back in the binder yesterday and this afternoon, when Dad went to make the pie."

"And where was the binder during that time?" Yasmeen asked.

"Mostly on the kitchen counter," I said. "Dad looks at it when he's cooking. The spaghetti recipe and the cake recipe are both in it."

Yasmeen frowned. "Shoot, Alex. Everyone we know was in your kitchen last night."

"And lots of people were looking at Dad's recipes. Mrs. Aaron was, and Mrs. Ryan . . ."

"Your uncle Scott, too," Yasmeen said. "It looks like everyone had the opportunity."

I shook my head. "I already hate this investigation. I don't want the thief to be someone we know, someone we invited to my mom's birthday party."

"If there's one thing we've learned about detecting, Alex, it's that we have to be objective," Yasmeen reminded me. "We can't decide somebody didn't do it just because they're friends or neighbors—or even relatives."

Yasmeen picked up the binder and opened it randomly to the recipe for Granddad's yam, marshmallow, and cornflake casserole. With Dad's recipes, you can see the ones he makes a lot because they are the most marked up and stained. This one had two orange spots—yams, probably—but he makes it only at Christmas, so overall it was pretty clean. Next, Yasmeen flipped to the recipes in the *Sweets* section. Like I said, my dad believes in recycling, and pretty much all the *Sweets* recipes were printed out on the flip side of used printer paper. The recipes are popular, and some were spotted all over.

"The pumpkin pie recipe would go here." Yasmeen turned again to the place between chocolate-cherry mousse and pitty-pink pudding. There was an old e-mail or something printed on the back of the mousse recipe, and there were three fresh smudges—one red and two blue—on the pitty-pink pudding recipe. "Look at this," Yasmeen said.

I nodded. "That red one is Luau's paw print from last night. The binder must have been lying open on the floor, and after Luau dived into the spaghetti, he ran over it on his way to the basement."

Dad stopped stirring and looked up. "Luau dived into the spaghetti?"

"Oh, yeah," I said. "I guess we forgot to tell you."

"And I guess I won't be serving leftovers for dinner," Dad said.

I looked back at the recipes. "That explains the red smudge, but what about these blue ones?"

While we were talking, Luau, who had recovered from last night's embarrassment, had strolled into the kitchen and jumped up on the table. He is not supposed to be there, but I was too distracted to put him down.

Yasmeen shook her head. "Ink, maybe? It's not like there're a lot of blue foods."

Luau doesn't like to be ignored. He stepped onto the binder, sniffed, widened his yellow eyes, and looked up at me: *Yummy!*

"Hey, buddy, get off the evidence, would you?"

I tried to shove him to one side, but he wouldn't go. Instead, he waved his tail like a flag, circled around, and bumped his head against the binder: *Did I mention: "Yummy"?*

Yasmeen looked at me. "What's with your feline, Alex?"

At first I had no clue, but then I got it. "Cheesy Deans! That's the blue stuff—Luau can smell it."

"Of course!" Yasmeen nodded. "So whoever was looking at these recipes must have had Cheesy Dean powder on his fingers—or on her fingers."

"So who was eating Cheesy Deans?"

We thought back to last night, and the people we remembered eating them were Uncle Scott and Zooey Bonjour.

"Mr. Stone ate some, too," Yasmeen said, "but only to be polite. Plus he likes to cook. Zooey Bonjour said his hot chocolate is the best."

"But Mr. Stone's our neighbor!" I protested.

"Didn't Michael Jensen eat some Cheesy Deans?" Yasmeen asked.

"You're right," I said. "He liked 'em."

"So let me get this straight," Dad said. "Are the people who ate Cheesy Deans your suspects—the potential recipe thief? Because if so, I think we can rule out your uncle. Kate says he can't even make instant oatmeal."

"Zooey Bonjour is a chef—which means, of course, she's interested in recipes," Yasmeen said.

"So based on means, motive, and opportunity, Zooey Bonjour would be our Number One suspect," I said.

Dad shook his head. "I know Zooey ran into some trouble once, but I'll never believe she's a thief."

This was the second time I'd heard about Zooey Bonjour's "trouble." I asked Dad what it was, but all he'd say is what I already knew: For a while Zooey didn't have her TV show, and then she got it back.

I looked at Yasmeen and knew she was thinking the

same as me—that we needed to talk someplace where Dad wasn't listening. I was counting on her to think of a way for us to make our exit, and pretty soon she did— only it wasn't exactly what I had in mind.

"I think before we investigate anybody, we should go through the trash," she said.

"*What?*"

"There's a chance the recipe got thrown away by mistake," she said. "We'll start with the kitchen. Ready?"

If you ever thought it would be glamorous to be a detective, you should've spent the next half hour with Yasmeen and me going through all the wastebaskets in my house and then through the party trash. And what did we get for our trouble? Totally, thoroughly, and absolutely disgusted with day-old spaghetti, chocolate cake, and sticky, melted vanilla ice cream.

We didn't find any recipes. But, without Dad listening, we did decide on step one of our investigation: We would use our secret weapon! So later, while we were washing our hands in the downstairs bathroom, Yasmeen asked if I wanted to eat over.

"You bet!" I love eating dinner at the Popps' house. And besides, it looked like Dad's dinner plan—leftover spaghetti—wasn't exactly going to work out.

Chapter Eight

When Yasmeen and I say "secret weapon," we mean her mom: Anita Popp, ace librarian. She works at the college, and she reads *everything*. Anything she doesn't know, she can find out.

It's always good to eat dinner at the Popps' house, but it's especially good on Sunday. That night, Mrs. Popp made fried chicken, creamed corn, biscuits, and sliced tomatoes. Professor Popp said grace before we ate, and into the prayer he inserted a special welcome to me: "We are blessed to share our bounty this evening with our neighbor Alex Parakeet." Professor Popp has an echoey voice and a cool accent from the Caribbean island where he grew up. Even if he's only saying "Pass the biscuits, please," he sounds smart.

"Your father's pie looks delicious, Alex," Mrs. Popp said once everyone had been served. "I am so impressed with his cooking! Is he looking forward to his TV appearance?"

"Not exactly." I explained about the missing recipe and how the pie I had brought over was one of Dad's experiments. "But he only has till Saturday to get the recipe right," I said.

Jeremiah shook his head and frowned. "Uh-oh."

"I infer," Professor Popp said, "that you and Yasmeen are detecting again."

"That's right," Yasmeen said. "And we have a question for you, Mom. Do you remember ever reading anything about 'trouble' involving Zooey Bonjour?"

"You don't think Zooey Bonjour has anything to do with the missing recipe, do you?" Mrs. Popp asked. "She has such lovely manners!"

"She probably doesn't," I said, "but we have to start somewhere."

"I seem to remember, Anita, that there was a scandal involving Ms. Bonjour several years ago," Professor Popp said.

A scandal?

Mrs. Popp shook her head. "It's best not to speculate when someone's reputation is involved. Let's wait till after dinner and get the facts right."

At the Popps' house there's a rule that dinner conversation must be about topics of general interest that won't interfere with digestion. That's why sometimes no one can think of anything to say.

I was trying to decide between eating another bite of corn and another bite of biscuit when Professor Popp broke the silence. "Didn't Yasmeen say something about your aunt visiting your history class tomorrow, Alex?"

"That's right," I said. "You know she has that website called WereYouontheMayflower.com. It's got a lot of historical information, so it's popular with teachers, especially around Thanksgiving."

Professor Popp smiled. "I believe we can be pretty certain—even without a visit to the website—that our ancestors were *not* on the *Mayflower*."

Most of the time I don't think about how Yasmeen's family is African American and mine is white. I knew from Yasmeen that Mrs. Popp's ancestors were slaves who picked cotton in Mississippi, and Professor Popp's were slaves who worked on sugar plantations on that Caribbean island, wherever it was. I was pretty sure there were no black people on the *Mayflower*.

"Why do people care if their ancestors came to America on some old boat?" Jeremiah asked. With most six-year-olds, you'd probably have to explain about the Pilgrims coming to Massachusetts on the *Mayflower* in 1620, but Jeremiah, being a genius, already knew all that.

"That is an excellent question," Professor Popp said, as if he were talking to one of his classes at the college. "What do you think, Yasmeen?"

Yasmeen thought for a moment. "I guess since there aren't any kings and queens in the United States, knowing your ancestors came over a long time ago is the next best thing. It shows you have class—sort of like a poodle that has a pedigree."

"There are many websites about African American ancestry, too," Mrs. Popp said. "People want to believe they are special. Having interesting ancestors is one way to demonstrate that."

"But everybody has *some* kind of interesting ancestors," I said. "In my family, they were farmers. In Bub's, they were coal miners. It's not like they were kings and queens, but it's still cool to think about."

Professor Popp said, "Very good, Mr. Parakeet." Then Mrs. Popp said, "I believe it's best to feel special for what you accomplish yourself," and then Yasmeen said, speaking of farmers, was the corn we were eating what we had harvested at Aaron Farm in the summer?

Mrs. Popp said it was. She had cut the kernels off the cob and frozen them. Professor Popp asked if Mrs. Aaron's business stayed busy in the fall, and I told him that a lot of visitors who come for football games stop at the farm store. After that, we talked about football for a while. Even Yasmeen's family, which is usually so brainy and calm, gets excited over Knightly Tiger football. Finally, Yasmeen and I cleared the plates, and then it was time for pie.

Dad had already sampled a piece of this one and

pronounced it tasty . . . but not quite as tasty as million-dollar pumpkin pie. Even so, no one at the Popps' house left a crumb.

Yasmeen and I loaded the dishwasher while Mrs. Popp went on the computer to look up the information about Zooey Bonjour and "trouble."

"I think I've found out what you wanted to know," Mrs. Popp said when we walked into the office.

Yasmeen asked, "Who did she poison?"

"Yasmeen!" I said.

"It only makes sense!" Yasmeen insisted. "How else does a cook get in trouble?"

"It's never wise to jump to conclusions, Yasmeen," Mrs. Popp said. "Sit down, and I'll tell you."

Yasmeen and I each took a chair, and Mrs. Popp began. "Zooey Bonjour's trouble started when people found out she wasn't born 'Zooey Bonjour.' In fact, her real name is Margaret Drebelbeis."

"There's an Ike Drebelbeis in my math class," I said.

Mrs. Popp nodded. "It's a common name in this region. Zooey and your grandmother grew up together over in Clear Meadow—not so far away."

"Drebelbeis doesn't sound very French," Yasmeen said.

"And for her, that was the problem," Mrs. Popp said. "Traditionally, great cooks have been French. She thought people would take her more seriously if she had a French name. She thought it might help her find work."

"So she called herself 'Bonjour' because it sounded French," I said. "But there's nothing really wrong with changing your name, is there? Like rap singers and movie stars do it all the time."

Mrs. Popp nodded. "True. But Zooey went further than that. As she started climbing the career ladder, she added a few credentials to her résumé that she didn't really possess."

Credentials to her résumé? I had no idea what Mrs. Popp was talking about. But I would never admit that with Yasmeen in the room.

"What credentials?" Yasmeen asked.

"Well, according to this story in the food section of the *Times*, she claimed she had graduated from a famous French cooking school when, in fact, she had not," Mrs. Popp said. "And she said she had cooked with some of the most famous chefs in France, but those stories didn't check out, either."

"She lied!" I said.

"That's terrible," Yasmeen said.

"It's wrong," Mrs. Popp agreed. "But it's common. People lie to get a job, to protect themselves—sometimes just so other people will think they're special."

"And when people found out who she really was, then what happened?" I asked.

Mrs. Popp turned back to the computer. "It's pretty much the way I remembered it," she said after a minute. "The EAT network canceled her show, but by then her viewers loved her. So many complained that the network gave her another chance. There's one story here about how she came clean and apologized to her fans— even cried right on television. And now"—Mrs. Popp turned to face us again—"Zooey Bonjour is more popular than ever."

I looked at Yasmeen. "Her fans forgave her," I said, "and so should we."

Yasmeen wasn't convinced. "Think about it, bud," she said. "If it turns out she stole your dad's pie recipe, could we forgive her for that?"

Chapter Nine

It wasn't until Monday morning that it really hit me: My crazy, fast-talking, whirlwind aunt was coming to *my* school. What if she showed up in a turkey costume?

By the time I got to homeroom, my stomach was churning the way it does before a visit to the dentist. Aunt Kate was speaking in the library, and at nine thirty my history teacher walked our class over there. I saw Aunt Kate right away and was relieved to see she was dressed normal—not even a Pilgrim hat. But then Mrs. Delafield, the librarian, introduced Aunt Kate and said I was her nephew, and a lot of kids nudged each other and looked over at me.

I wanted to sink through the floor.

Aunt Kate started out telling how important the *Mayflower* was in American history. Then she told about the first Thanksgiving, when the Native Americans and the Pilgrims ate together to celebrate the harvest and being alive after so many people had died.

Once the history part was done, she used PowerPoint to show us how to use WereYouontheMayflower.com.

Then we all got to sit down at the computers and try it ourselves.

What you do is type in your name and birthday, then follow prompts that ask for more information, like the names of grandparents and great-grandparents as far back as you know, and also their hometowns, and the year they were born. You go through a whole bunch of screens this way, each one asking more questions but also with pictures and historical information.

At the end, either you get to a screen that says, "YES! There is an excellent chance that you are descended from [name of ancestor], who was aboard the *Mayflower*," or you get a screen that says, "SO SORRY! Our records indicate you probably did not have an ancestor on the *Mayflower*."

Everybody knew Aunt Kate was coming today, so some of the brainiac kids had brought information about their relatives. Aunt Kate explained that the more you know, the better the computer's answer is, but either way she couldn't promise it was totally right. "This is really just a starting place for more research," she said. "Many times, after people go to our website, they get hooked on genealogy—learning about who your ancestors were and what they did."

Aunt Kate had already done a search on our own family, so I knew I didn't have a *Mayflower* ancestor on my dad's side. When I got my turn at the computer, I tried my mom's family, entering the names of my grandparents and whatever else I could remember about them. Eventually, I got the "Sorry" screen, which is what everybody sitting around me got, too. But sitting at a terminal down the row from me was Tanner Whittaker, and suddenly he shouted, "Yes!" and a bunch of us went over to look.

Sure enough, the screen was telling him that he might be descended from Giles Hopkins, who was just a little older than us when he came over on the *Mayflower* with his father, Stephen, and his stepmother, Elizabeth.

After that, the bell rang, and it was time to go to our next class. I was just thinking how Aunt Kate's visit had turned out fine—everybody seemed to think she was cool, even—when she came up and spoiled everything by giving me a big hug and a lipstick kiss. She was going for my cheek, I think, but she got my ear all red-smudged instead. *Yuck.*

"Great to see you, kiddo!" she said. "And don't forget, I'm staying for lunch!"

While Aunt Kate made a presentation to the seventh graders, I went to math. After that came lunch, and Yasmeen and I met her in the caf. No kid in the history of my school has ever tried the cafeteria meat loaf, but Aunt Kate did and said it was *"Great!"* She also ate every one of her cherry Jell-O cubes. When she mentioned that she and Uncle Scott were having dinner with Zooey and Grandma that night, Yasmeen told her about the missing recipe and the secret ingredient.

"Dad hired us to investigate," I said.

"But doesn't your dad at least remember the ingredient?" Aunt Kate asked. Then, before I could say anything, she answered herself: "Oh, right. This is my brother we're talking about."

I defended my dad. "He remembers the code was like a crossword puzzle clue, and it said 'two words.' "

"Oh, was it one of Great-grandma Bea's recipes?" Aunt Kate asked. "She died when I was a baby, but everyone always told me she was a crossword puzzle fiend. Do you know anybody like that? Maybe they could help."

Yasmeen and I looked at each other. "Mr. Lee!" we said at the same time.

Aunt Kate didn't know who that was, so I explained. "Remember Toby from the party? The kid who popped the balloons? Mr. Lee's his dad. He travels all the time, and on airplanes he does crossword puzzles."

Aunt Kate nodded. "If I had that kid, I'd travel all the time, too."

The first bell rang, and lunch was over. Aunt Kate kissed us both good-bye—*Yuck*. Walking to our lockers, Yasmeen and I made a plan to phone Mr. Lee, but it would have to wait till after dinner. At 3:15, Dad was picking us up from school to take us out to Aaron Farm to volunteer, same as he does every Monday.

My mom calls the farm "the last refuge for hippies in College Springs," and my dad says that's exactly why it's a wonderful place for a dirt-loving kid. Besides vegetables, there's a nasty old barn cat to catch the mice, and there are a couple of happy, smelly dogs to bark and chase groundhogs. There's also a gift shop where you can buy jam and seeds and vegetables and plants and earrings. Mrs. Aaron says the gift shop's where the real money is—or where the real money would be if she could ever figure out exactly what she ought to be selling.

It was never my idea to go to work on a vegetable farm, but after baseball ended last summer, I didn't have that much to do, and Dad started thinking my face would turn gray-green from playing Lousy Luigi III. Also, I guess he heard from Mom that the farm wasn't doing so well and that Mrs. Aaron was hoping to trade vegetables for help. Dad talked to Yasmeen's mom, and the next thing we knew, Yasmeen and I were going out there once a week.

At first, I didn't like it so much. Dad tried to tell me farm chores aren't like house chores, but I guess I know work when I see it, and picking corn and beans and pulling weeds are work. My muscles hurt, my hands got blisters, and I got a sunburn on my neck. Plus, the first time I got assigned to do weeding, I pulled all the dill plants by mistake.

Oops.

After a while, though, I learned the difference between weeds and herbs, the dogs started wagging their tails, and the cat stopped hissing. Now my hands are calloused and my muscles don't hurt, and sometimes I kind of look forward to being outside. Plus Mrs. Aaron always gives us a treat when the work's done.

Dad dropped Yasmeen and me off and reminded us to bring home plenty of pumpkins. This did not turn out to be a problem. We had barely greeted the smelly dogs when Mrs. Aaron assigned us to harvest the last of them, and for the next two hours, Yasmeen and I pulled pumpkins of all sizes and shapes off vines, carried them to a wagon hitched to a tractor, and loaded them in.

While we worked, we argued. Yasmeen had talked herself into believing Zooey Bonjour had stolen the recipe.

"She lied about her past," Yasmeen said.

"Lying doesn't make someone a thief," I said.

"But it means she has a criminal mind!" Yasmeen said. "Plus there's the other evidence. She looked at the binder at your mom's party. As far as we know, she's the last person to have seen the pie recipe before it disappeared. Plus didn't we say it was probably someone with a purse who stole it?"

By the time the last pumpkin was loaded, it was cold and almost dark. Mrs. Aaron laughed when she saw how beat up we were—streaked with dirt and saggy-tired. "Thanks a million, you two," she said. "Come on into the workroom, and I'll give you some cider."

In the workroom, there's a rickety old table, a woodstove, and a desk. When it's cold, Mrs. Aaron keeps a pot of cider on the stove—to drink and also because it makes the whole shop smell good for the customers. Now she ladled out mugs of hot cider for all three of us, and we sat down to drink it.

Mrs. Aaron has brown hair with streaks of gray that she usually tucks up under a baseball cap. She had dressed up for the party, but today she was wearing dusty jeans, a sweatshirt, and workboots—along with a pair of the dangly earrings she sells in the gift shop.

"What was it your dad told me about a missing recipe when he phoned?" Mrs. Aaron asked.

A bad thing about investigating is that you get suspicious of everybody. No way did I think Mrs. Aaron was a thief, but still. . . . She had been one of the people in the kitchen at the party. Would she want to take away my dad's chance of being on TV?

Yasmeen explained it was the Thanksgiving pie recipe that was gone. "You were looking at the binder at the party, weren't you?" Yasmeen asked. "Did you notice whether the pumpkin pie recipe was there then?"

Mrs. Aaron answered the question with a question. "Were the recipes in alphabetical order?"

I explained my dad's filing system.

"Then it was already gone by the time I saw the binder," Mrs. Aaron said.

"Really?" Yasmeen set her mug down on the table. "Are you sure?"

Mrs. Aaron nodded. "I was looking for it specifically. I wanted to see how much pumpkin the pie required. When I didn't see the recipe, I figured I didn't understand how they were organized, or else it was out of order. Anyway, other people wanted to see the recipes, so I didn't have much time to think about it."

The sweet, hot cider was definitely making my muscles feel better, plus I think it was improving my brainpower. Now we could narrow down when the recipe had disappeared.

"If your dad can't find the recipe, does that mean he won't be on *The Zooey Bonjour Show*?" Mrs. Aaron asked.

Did she say it in a hopeful way? I couldn't be sure. But I told her Dad was experimenting with lots of pies. "That's one reason he needs so many pumpkins," I said.

Mrs. Aaron looked thoughtful. "I wonder if Zooey Bonjour ever had a chance to try that apricot-okra chutney I sell at the store. I don't mind telling you I'd like to be on a show like hers. It could bring customers to Aaron Farm. This year's been a tough one. I'm not sure how much longer I can hold out."

"Hold out?" Yasmeen repeated.

"Stay in business . . . stay in my house, even," Mrs. Aaron said. "I owe money on the land and on the equipment, and I've got to buy seeds for next year if I expect to have a harvest. It's not so easy running a small farm on your own. You need to take every advantage."

I don't know what happened to Mr. Aaron, but Mrs. Aaron lives by herself. It was terrible to think of her losing her farm, maybe even her house. I told her I was sorry. Just then I heard the *crunch* of a car on the gravel outside—Dad coming to get us.

Mrs. Aaron heard the car, too. She set her mug down, stretched, and stood up. "Things have a way of working out," she said. "In the meantime, let's gather up those pumpkins and get you two on your way."

Outside, Dad popped the trunk of the car, and we piled pie pumpkins inside.

"Those ought to keep me busy for a while," Dad told Mrs. Aaron.

She answered something about being busy herself,

and while the two of them chatted, Yasmeen and I got into the car, Yasmeen riding shotgun and me in the back. The second the door slammed, Yasmeen looked over her shoulder and said, "We need to talk about this latest development in the case!"

"What latest development?"

Yasmeen checked to make sure Dad and Mrs. Aaron were still talking. Then she said: "It's Mrs. Aaron! I'm positive. *She's* the one who stole the recipe!"

Chapter Ten

Dad climbed into the car about a half second later, so there was no time to ask Yasmeen what in heck she was talking about, or to remind her that she had spent, like, the whole afternoon trying to convince me that Zooey Bonjour was the recipe thief. Yasmeen was right about one thing, though. We needed to talk. So I asked my dad if she could stay for dinner, and he said he had been about to suggest the same thing.

"In fact, I have a job for you guys—a paying job, if you're interested."

Paying? "We're interested," I said.

"You remember all those notes our neighbors wrote to Zooey the other night?" Dad asked. "The ones about the food? Well, Grandma's assistant was supposed to organize them, but he's got the flu. She knows how responsible you guys are and wondered if you'd do it."

"It sounds easier than pulling pumpkins," I said. "How much?"

"Alex, don't be crass," Yasmeen said. "And if you're wondering what 'crass' means, it's—"

"Actually, I wasn't wondering," I said.

"You'll have to negotiate that with your grandmother," Dad said. "She dropped the notes and the files off this afternoon. Could you do it tonight? How's the homework situation?"

"No homework," I said. "And we can talk to Mr. Lee tomorrow." We had already told Dad about Aunt Kate's idea. I leaned forward and whispered to Yasmeen. "Do you want to check what's for dinner first? In case it's something weird?"

"I heard that," Dad said.

Oops.

"I'm sure dinner will be delicious," Yasmeen said politely. "Uh . . . but what is it, by the way?"

Dad explained he had turned one of his pie crusts into a quiche—which is pronounced "keesh" and ought to be spelled that way, too. A quiche is like a cheese and egg pie. It's pretty good if there's bacon in it. But I knew from bitter experience that sometimes Dad uses perfectly decent cheese to disguise highly undesirable vegetables.

"What did you put in this one?" I asked, trying to make my voice sound curious instead of suspicious.

Dad smiled at me in the rearview mirror. "Don't worry—you'll love it!" he said.

Uh-oh.

When we got to my house, Yasmeen called her parents, and they said she could stay. Dad was taking the quiche out of the oven when Yasmeen came into the kitchen. I sniffed to see if I could detect questionable ingredients, then I told Yasmeen she was a brave woman.

Dad yanked a dish towel from its hook. "Insult my quiche, will you?" He turned to me like a fencer. *"En garde!"* He snapped the towel in front of my face.

I grabbed another dish towel, and snapped it back.

"Touché!" Dad said, and we jumped and danced around the kitchen, thrusting and parrying with dish towel swords.

Playing the part of Mom, Yasmeen shook her head and rolled her eyes.

Finally, we were both out of breath, and Dad waved his towel and said, "Truce! I need to make a salad. And you need to feed your cat."

"Okay," I said, "but this doesn't mean I surrender. Where is Luau, anyway?"

Being proud of his big furry tummy, Luau does not like to miss meals. Usually, I feed him at six o'clock, and usually, he's rubbing my legs and meowing by 5:55. The stove clock said 6:10 now.

"Luau!?" I called.

Yasmeen cocked her head. "I think I hear him."

She was right. Very faintly, I heard a sleepy answering *Mrrrow*.

"It's coming from the basement," I said. Following Yasmeen, I clomped down the stairs. At the bottom, relaxing in the recycling bin, was Luau. He blinked a long slow blink, tilted his head back, and yawned, which meant, *What's all the racket about?*

"What are you doing down here?" I knelt and scratched his ears. "You never hang out in the recycling. Don't you want dinner?"

Luau head-bumped my hand, arched his back, and stretched. *Is it that time already?* Then he jumped lightly out of the bin and started climbing the stairs.

I turned to follow, but Yasmeen said, "Hey, bud—look at this." She was pointing at the newspaper on top of the stack in the bin. It was the Saturday sports section, and the headline read, "Tigers Favored to Claw Minnesota."

"What? You think we should save it in a scrapbook?" I asked.

"No, not the paper—what's *on* the paper," Yasmeen said. "There are blue smudges—just like the ones in the recipe binder!"

I was halfway upstairs, but that got my attention. I went back and looked in the bin. Sure enough, there was a single blue smudge on each side of the page, like someone's blurred thumbprints.

"That must be why Luau's hanging out here all of a sudden," I said. "With his amazing nose, he can smell like a single molecule of Cheesy Deans."

Yasmeen gave me the steady look that means the wheels in her brain are spinning. "Bud," she said, "I have an idea. We know the missing pie recipe has Cheesy Dean smudges on it, too, right? So in that case, what if Luau could help us solve the crime? What if we got him near the missing recipe, and he sniffed it out—like a bloodhound?"

"Brilliant, Yasmeen," I said. "Except for one little problem: We don't know where the missing recipe is. I mean, that's kind of the meaning of 'missing.'"

My logic did not impress my detecting partner. "She must have it in her workroom," she said thoughtfully. "That's where she keeps her files. So all we have to do is sneak Luau in . . . and he finds it."

"Who's 'she'? Mrs. Aaron? But who says she took the recipe?" I asked.

"I do!" Yasmeen said. "She wants her own chance to be on *Zooey Bonjour* with that vegetable chutney stuff. She's hoping millions of Zooey's viewers will order it, and she can make enough money to save her farm. Didn't she say she had to 'take every advantage'? She practically confessed!"

From the top of the stairs came a sad meow: *As usual, my needs have been forgotten.*

Yasmeen looked up at my cat and spoke in a wheedling voice. "Come on, kitty—you want to help us solve this mystery, don't you?"

Luau stuck his nose in the air and made a whisker adjustment that meant, *If that's what a fellow has to do to get fed around here. . . .*

Back upstairs, I measured out Luau's food and dumped it into his bowl. I didn't want to admit it, but what Yasmeen said about Mrs. Aaron kind of made sense. There was no time to talk about it now, though. I heard the squeak of the garage door opening. Dad heard it, too, and said, "Mom's home! Time for dinner!"

Dinner at my house is nothing like dinner at Yasmeen's. We eat at the kitchen table, not in the dining room. We don't say grace. We use paper napkins, the plates don't necessarily match, and sometimes my dad drinks a beer right out of the bottle.

The only rule about conversation is no jokes about body stuff.

"The quiche is delicious, Mr. Parakeet," Yasmeen said.

"Is there bacon in this?" I asked. "And that looks like broccoli. Is that broccoli?"

"Eat it, don't analyze it," my mom said.

"Have you seen the new sportswriters' poll?" Dad asked, changing the subject. "The Tigers are ranked number five in their division!"

The Ohio team, it turned out, was ranked number four, so the game this coming weekend was extra-important. If the Tigers won, they might get to play in the postseason.

"Zooey's show should have even more viewers than usual, then," Dad said. "It'll be a lead-in to the game since they're broadcasting from outside the stadium."

"Speaking of the show," Mom said. "I saw Zooey downtown this afternoon with Ted Stone."

"Might be a little romance brewing there," Dad said. "He seems quite smitten. I understand he's taking both Zooey and my mom to the women's volleyball game up on campus tomorrow afternoon."

A few bites later, Mom asked how the recipe search was going. Yasmeen and I looked at each other and, without saying anything, agreed we wouldn't mention either Zooey Bonjour or Mrs. Aaron. Instead, I told her about our plan to talk to Mr. Lee.

"You'll have to wait for a rare moment when he's home, then," Dad said.

Mom shook her head. "I can't believe I forgot to tell you. He's home right now—on his own with the kids till

Wednesday night! Marjie left yesterday for some kind of family nutrition class in Florida."

Dad actually dropped his fork. *"What?"*

Mom laughed. "She told me about it at the party Saturday. Full-time with a baby and a toddler just about put her over the edge. She told her husband she needed a break, or else. I wonder how he's doing with them."

Dad cupped his hand to his ear. "No bloodcurdling screams."

Maybe not, but later, when dinner was over and I went to call him, Mr. Lee didn't sound so good. I let it go eight rings and he didn't answer, so I hung up. Ten seconds later he called back, out of breath.

"Sorry—so sorry," he said. "I finally found the phone in the drier. Toby must've put it there, or maybe I was getting the laundry and—*Hey, wait! Give that back!*"

I heard a baby's wail, a *crack* that probably meant the phone had been dropped, then a bunch of *thump*s. Finally, Mr. Lee's voice came back, shouting over the noise of a baby crying. "Sorry—so sorry. Toby thinks it's the height of hilarious to steal his sister's binky right out of her mouth—then he runs for it."

"Did you get the binky back?" I asked.

"Not yet." From the way his voice sounded, I could tell he was bouncing Baby Alex. "Last time, he buried it in a houseplant."

I felt bad asking Mr. Lee for a favor at a time like this, but he said he'd be happy to tell us everything he knew about crosswords. "Besides, it'll be good to talk to people whose vocabulary exceeds fifty words," he said.

Yasmeen and I still had the job for Grandma to do, so I told him we'd be over the next night, Tuesday, after dinner. Of course, maybe by then Dad would have experimented his way to the pumpkin pie recipe and we wouldn't need Mr. Lee's help at all. But either way, it sounded as though maybe Mr. Lee could use ours.

Chapter Eleven

Back in the kitchen, Mom and Yasmeen were finishing the dishes. Dad had left for the grocery store. His plan was to scan the shelves of the baking aisle, hoping some item would jog his memory about the secret ingredient. If that didn't work, he'd buy every possible two-word food you could stir into a pumpkin pie.

The best place to work on Grandma's project was the kitchen table, so I wiped up the crumbs and Yasmeen retrieved what we needed from the hall. There was a giant plastic box containing file folders, an inkpad and a rubber stamp with the date on it, and a big envelope containing the notes from Saturday night, which were handwritten on lined paper. There was also a typed sheet of instructions for us from Grandma.

The job reminded me of organizing Dad's recipe binder. After we stamped each page, we were supposed to put it in the right folder—like *Desserts—Pie* or *Appetizers—Dip* or *Salads—Fruit*. Of course, there was no way now for Zooey actually to taste the food. But Grandma's instructions explained that when Zooey needed an idea for a show, she would look through this box for inspiration, and if something looked good, she'd call and ask the cook for details.

I thought the job would take about ten minutes, but it was actually tricky. Like, not everybody has easy-to-read handwriting. And sometimes it was hard to decide on the right category. Was Beth Ryan's lime Jell-O marshmallow fluff a dessert or a salad? And what about Mrs. Jensen's potato doughnuts—bread, breakfast, or pastry?

Being the daughter of a librarian, Yasmeen came up with the idea of "cross-referencing." So with the fluff, we put the actual note under *Salad,* but then we put a short note of our own under *Dessert,* saying that there was a fluff recipe under *Salad.*

You can imagine this all took a while, but finally we got down to the last few and saw that among them was a page that was different—a piece of stationery with a blue border. At the top of the sheet was the number 2, so we knew it was the second page of something. When I flipped it over, the back was blank.

"Take a look at this one," I said to Yasmeen, and we both read together:

> . . . *so gratified you've invited me to appear on your upcoming Pennsylvania show. I don't mind telling you I've been a big fan of yours for several years now. Since*

I've been living on my own, I've turned to the EAT network many times for cooking tips. In particular, your recipe for chicken paprika has been a lifesaver anytime I . . .

I grabbed the rest of the papers and looked through them. "No page three," I said, "and no page one."

"Even so," Yasmeen said. "It's pretty obvious what this means. It was never Mrs. Aaron at all. Zooey Bonjour is *definitely* our recipe thief."

Yasmeen might be my best friend who happens to be a girl, but sometimes—like now—she is exasperating. "Would you please make up your mind?" I said. "One second it's totally one person, and the next it's totally somebody else!"

Yasmeen was exasperated, too. "Well, that's better than you, at least. You don't want it to be anybody!"

"Of course I don't," I said. "I like Zooey Bonjour. And I like Mrs. Aaron. Why would I want either of them to have stolen something my dad needs?"

"It's not a matter of who we like; it's a matter of solving the case," Yasmeen said. "And this letter clinches it. *Duh.*"

Usually I never admit when I don't know what Yasmeen is talking about. But this time I was so annoyed I didn't even bother pretending. "*Duh* yourself," I said.

"I only hope Miss Popp doesn't mind enlightening those of us who lack her superior intellect."

Big surprise—Yasmeen said she'd be happy to.

"The letter's from Mr. Stone," she declared. 'Living on my own'—that's the clue. Mr. Stone's wife is dead, right? Zooey must have invited him to be on the show instead of your dad, and this is his reply. She must want him to make hot chocolate."

"But why wouldn't Zooey just *un*-invite my dad in that case?" I said. "Why go to so much trouble?"

"I don't know for sure," Yasmeen admitted, "but it's probably because of your grandma. It would be awkward for Zooey to tell her friend's son he couldn't be on the show. But if the recipe is gone and Zooey has to un-invite him, then it doesn't look like it was Zooey's fault."

I thought for a minute. "But even if you're right, I still don't get it. Why invite Mr. Stone?"

"Zooey said that his hot chocolate was the best she ever tasted—remember? And anyway, it's not just the recipes, bud. It's Mr. Stone himself. I think Zooey's falling in love with him!"

Love? Oh, *yuck*! I did not want to be having this conversation. So I picked up the next note and read aloud, "My recipe for 'pickled prune pie' was passed down from my great-grandmother to—"

"Alex!" Yasmeen reached for the paper. "I know you don't want to believe it, but it makes sense."

It didn't make sense to me, so—for a while—I kept arguing. Like, hadn't all this love stuff between Zooey Bonjour and Mr. Stone happened too fast to be for real? And anyway, why couldn't Zooey just invite Mr. Stone to be on another show later?

But Yasmeen had an answer for everything. Love happens fast all the time, she said. Hadn't I ever read *Romeo and Juliet*? (No, actually.) And the EAT network sends Zooey all over the country to do shows. It's not like she could just come to College Springs any old time she wanted. She might not do another show here for years.

"But even if she did steal the recipe, what can we do about it?" I said.

"The recipe must be in Zooey's room at the Knightly Tiger Inn, right?" Yasmeen said. "So our job is to take Luau over there and let him sniff it out."

We were both quiet for a couple of minutes, thinking the same thing: How to get ourselves—and Luau—into Grandma and Zooey's suite at the Knightly Tiger Inn when they weren't there.

"Wait a sec," I said. "Didn't Dad say Grandma and Zooey are going to the volleyball game with Mr. Stone tomorrow afternoon?"

Yasmeen nodded. "That's right. But we still need to figure out—"

"I've got it," I interrupted. "The televisions!"

Yasmeen closed her mouth and looked at me like I was crazy. "Televisions?"

"You know—the new TVs at the Knightly Tiger Inn! Aunt Kate was talking about them at the party. Anyway, tomorrow's Tuesday. The Knightly Tiger coaches' show is on at four. I can tell Grandma I'm dying to come over and watch all those highlight clips on one of those new TVs."

"Who would believe that?" Yasmeen asked.

"Watch this." I said.

My grandma's number is programmed into our home phone, so it was easy to pick up the phone and dial. Grandma answered on the first ring, and after the hellos, she asked if we were done organizing the notes.

"Notes?" I said. "Oh—*those* notes! Almost done. Uh . . . since you mention it, what's the usual pay for a job like that—in Hollywood, anyway?"

"I don't know what it is in Hollywood," Grandma replied, "but in College Springs it's twenty-five dollars for each of you. Does that sound fair?"

I mouthed "twenty-five" to Yasmeen, and she gave me a thumbs-up sign.

"That sounds great," I said. "But I have another question." I told her what I wanted, and she went for it immediately. She's a TV professional, after all. Then she said she and Zooey would be gone—which of course I already knew—and she would leave a key for me at the front desk.

I thanked her and hung up. Then I looked at Yasmeen. "Told ya."

It was a few minutes after Yasmeen went home that I heard Dad come back from the store. I met him in the kitchen. "Any luck?"

"Nothing obvious," Dad said, "but plenty of possibilities. Anyway, I have my work cut out for me. I have to start cooking for Thanksgiving on Wednesday. Till then, it's gonna be pies and more pies." He yawned and added, "Maybe I'll use Mom's new coffeemaker to brew a big pot now. I'm not expecting to get much sleep."

Chapter Twelve

That night, I dreamed of pumpkin pie.

And when the alarm went off and Luau head-bumped my face, I smelled pumpkin pie. Only when I got up did I realize it was no dream. My room really did smell like pumpkin pie.

So did the hallway. So did the bathroom.

Brushed, dressed, and ready to face the day, I walked into the kitchen a few minutes later. The table, the counters, and the stovetop were all piled with pumpkin pie.

Dad, wearing the same clothes he had on yesterday, was dozing in his chair. The oven timer was dinging.

"Dad, wake up!" I said.

Without opening his eyes, Dad shifted and mumbled, "Pepper flakes?"

I grabbed a couple of potholders, opened the oven door, and pulled out the latest pie. The timer must have been dinging for a while, because the crust was coffee-colored and the filling looked dried out and sad. I couldn't find spare surface space in the kitchen, so

I carried the pie to the family room to cool. There were already two on the coffee table.

Mom was in the kitchen when I returned. *"Oh, my gravy!"* she said. "How am I supposed to make coffee?!"

Her voice woke Dad, who almost jumped out of his chair. *"What?"* He looked at the clock. "The pie!"

"In the family room," I said.

Dad's face was anxious, like someone waiting for a doctor's diagnosis. "And?"

I shook my head. "One for the squirrels."

Breakfast was—guess what?—pumpkin pie. Dad said he was going to do a formal taste test later, but for now Mom and I could each take a piece of whatever looked good and give a report.

I took a bite and thought of cookies.

"Well?" Dad said.

"Are there chocolate chips in this pie?"

Dad nodded. "Melted into the custard."

"Chocolate?" Mom said. "I want some of that!"

"Trade you." I handed it over. "How's this one?"

"Well," Mom said, "I wouldn't say exactly *bad*."

I tried it and—*yuck!* "I would! What is it?"

"Orange marmalade," Dad said. "Not a hit, huh?"

"Bitter!" I tried to steal the chocolate one back, but Mom held on tight.

"What else you got?" I asked.

By the time Yasmeen rang our doorbell, I had sampled four pies, which made for a queasy bus ride to school. And it didn't help that Yasmeen thought we should try to work out the mystery ingredient for ourselves.

"We know it's two words, and from what you tried this morning, we can eliminate orange marmalade, chocolate chips, marshmallow fluff, and coconut milk," she said. "What about ginger ale?"

"Or cream cheese?" I tried.

"Ice cream!" she said.

"Apple juice!"

"Tomato soup!"

"Tomato soup?"

"There's a chocolate cake recipe with tomato soup. Honest," she said.

We came up with more ideas: cranberry sauce, Jell-O pudding, maple syrup. And then we kind of got carried away: frosted flakes, mashed potatoes, spaghetti sauce!

"Ranch dressing!" Yasmeen shouted as the bus pulled up to the school.

"Bubblegum!" I replied.

"Bubblegum is one word, bud."

"Sugarless bubblegum!" I said.

Yasmeen nodded. "That works."

By now, it was time to grab my backpack. We made a plan to meet at lunch. We still had to work out the details of our after-school visit to the Knightly Tiger Inn.

By lunchtime, my tummy had settled down, so I loaded up my tray with pizza, french fries, and applesauce. Then Yasmeen and I found a table. The second we sat, I started eating and Yasmeen started talking. "The way I see it, we still need a way to get to the Knightly Tiger Inn this afternoon. We can't exactly ask our parents for a ride."

"Not with Luau," I said. "And that's another problem. How do we sneak him into the hotel? They don't allow pets."

"We can borrow my mom's old tote bag," Yasmeen said. "People in hotels always have luggage."

"What if he meows?" I asked.

"Tell him not to! What's the point of all this cat conversation if it only goes one way?"

I said I'd try. "But just because I understand Luau, it doesn't mean I can tell him what to do."

"What a couple of lame babies!" The familiar voice came from over my right shoulder. "All we gotta do is stuff Luau in the tote bag and take him in a back door. But why are we taking a cat to the Knightly Tiger Inn, anyway? What are we detecting? What did I miss?"

Yasmeen and I had the same thought at the same time: *It can't be.*

But actually it was.

Behind us, Sofie Sikora was sitting at a table by herself. "I'm gonna come sit with you guys," she said. "It's not so comfortable twisting my neck around to hear everything you say."

A moment later, she slapped her tray down across from mine, and for the next few minutes proceeded to tell us everything going on in the life of Sofie Sikora.

It was almost time for the bell when she leaned toward me. "Alex?" She looked me in the eye. "You smell."

I blushed down to my toenails.

Yasmeen said, "Sofie, even if it's true, it's not a very nice thing to say."

"I didn't say he smelled *disgusting.* I just said he smelled. Actually," she sniffed me, "it's a *good* smell. Kind of like—"

"Pumpkin pie?" Yasmeen said.

Sofie said, *"Yeah!"* just as the first bell rang. We were just about to escape to fifth period when Sofie said, "Okay, so we all meet at my house at three thirty. Alex brings the cat. Yazzie brings the tote bag."

Yasmeen and I looked at each other. *"What?"*

Sofie shrugged. "My mom'll take us to the Knightly

Tiger Inn. I'll think of some story to tell her. I'm glad to be investigating again. My life was a little boring—not to mention I liked having my picture in the paper and being on TV when we solved the Uncle Sam case, even if those other girls' pictures were bigger than mine, everybody said so. My mom—"

"*Sofie!*" I interrupted. "We're gonna be tardy. Bye!"

Maybe you noticed that neither Yasmeen nor I exactly agreed to meet Sofie after school. But we both knew we'd be there. Sofie Sikora is the most annoying person ever. But she always comes through when we need her.

Chapter Thirteen

At 3:35, Yasmeen and I were in the backseat of the Sikoras' car.

"But I don't understand," Mrs. Sikora was saying as she drove toward the Knightly Tiger Inn. "Don't you need me to come in and fill out paperwork?"

As promised, Sofie had thought up a story. It was something about a special engineering class for girls being offered by the college. This was not as crazy as it sounds because the Knightly Tiger Inn is next to an engineering building on the campus.

"It's free," Sofie said. "I got a scholarship."

To me, it seemed totally obvious that Sofie was making this up as she went along, and I expected any second now her mom would pull over and demand the truth. But instead Mrs. Sikora said, "Isn't that nice? And are you and Alex taking the class, too, Yasmeen? But I guess I'm a little confused here—didn't Sofie say it's for girls?"

There was a moment of silence while I waited for Yasmeen, who is so much smarter than I am, to field this question. But then I glanced sideways and saw the panic in her eyes. No help there. And Sofie?

From the passenger seat, she looked around at me expectantly.

"Uh . . . my class is different," I said. "It's . . . uh"—I glanced down at the cat in my lap—"animal science! We're going to dissect cats!"

Luau dug his claws into my knees and said, *"Mrrrow!"* which meant, *Mrrrow!*

Sofie's mom gasped. Sofie covered her smile with her hand.

"*Ow*, Luau! What I meant was not *dissect*, exactly, but *examine*—we're going to *examine* cats. You know, like doctors—with a stethoscope and tongue depressors and that little hammer for reflexes and everything."

When you don't know what you're talking about, it's smart to just shut up. For proof, look at Yasmeen. She is the smartest person I know, and all the way to the Knightly Tiger Inn, she never said a word. I, on the other hand, kept talking nonstop, inventing all kinds of details about this phantom class, like how Luau had volunteered to be the patient and how next week we were doing dentistry on guinea pigs.

By the time Mrs. Sikora pulled up to the inn, Sofie had turned pink from the strain of containing her laughter. The instant the car drove away, she and

Yasmeen both doubled over. Luau did not see anything funny. He blinked an angry blink that meant, *How would you like it if I examined* you *with a little hammer and tongue depressors?*

"Okay, we have to maintain," Yasmeen said, wiping a tear from her cheek. "We have serious work to do here. But, gosh, Alex, when you said the part about hamster tonsils, I thought I'd die."

"I liked the part about eye charts for cats," Sofie said, "with little mice and birds on them."

"Well, you guys were no help!" I said.

"Because you did so well on your own," Sofie said. "I know my mom, and she didn't suspect a thing. Yazzie," she said, turning to Yasmeen, "give the bag over. We gotta put the feline fatty inside. I hope he fits."

Luau didn't like being called a "fatty," and he didn't like being stuffed in a tote bag, either. "It's only for a couple of minutes, bud. Keep still."

But Luau didn't. He meowed. He scratched. He howled. He thrashed so much that anyone watching would have thought the tote bag was possessed. Luckily, it was too cold for anybody to be hanging around on the sidewalk.

"Hand me the bag," Yasmeen said to me, "and get going, Alex. Sofie, you know where the back door is, right? I'll go with you. Alex can come around and let us in."

I handed the tote bag to Yasmeen, took a deep breath for courage, pulled the big heavy door open, and walked in. I had never been inside the Knightly Tiger Inn, but I knew it was fancy. What I noticed right away was shiny brass and dark wood, and, besides, it was really warm.

The woman behind the reception desk looked like a college student. She had blond hair pulled back in a ponytail, and she was wearing a black jacket and a tiger-striped scarf around her neck. There was a name tag pinned on the jacket: "Amber."

"Good afternoon," Amber said. "May I help you?"

I had rehearsed this part. "Good afternoon," I said. "Catherine Parakeet is my grandmother. I think she left a key for me."

"Room number?" Amber said.

Room number? I wanted to sink through the floor. Grandma had told me her room number, but I couldn't remember it. My face must've said *"Panic!"* because Amber adopted a sympathetic preschool-teacher type of voice. "Don't worry," she said. "I can look it up." She tapped at the computer in front of her, then said, "Parakeet, right?" and tapped some more. "Two forty-five. Okay, just a sec." She took a piece of plastic like a credit card, swiped it in a machine, and pushed it across the counter to me. "There you go, honey."

I looked at the card. Was that a key? I've only stayed

in a hotel two times in my life, and I never had a key of my own. "Thanks," I said uncertainly. Then I turned away from the desk and started walking.

"Uh, honey? The elevators are that way." Amber pointed.

I could feel that she was watching, so I turned in the direction she said, but where was I going, exactly? The inn was a lot bigger than I had thought. On the wall by the elevators, there was a map of the building. Besides the front door, it showed four exits.

With no idea which one Yasmeen and Sofie had chosen, I picked the closest. It seemed to take forever to get there, and the whole time walking down the hallway I was worried that somebody would stop me and ask what I was doing. Finally, I reached the door and pushed hard. The rush of cold air gave me goosebumps. I looked right and left but only saw some bushes up against the building and a few students in parkas. I was about to close the door and try another when one of the bushes said, "*Psst!* Alex! Over here!"

I jumped about a foot off the ground. But then Sofie's head appeared above the bush, and a second later the rest of Sofie, too. "Yasmeen's got Luau at the other door. We knew you'd mess up, so I came to find you. Did you at least get the key?"

"Yes, I got the key, and why did you think I'd mess

up? And why were you hiding? And nobody told me there's four different—"

Sofie grabbed my arm and tugged. "It's freezing out here, Alex. Come on." She dragged me into the building and down the hall toward the lobby.

"Wait! We can't go that way!" I didn't want to walk past Amber again.

Sofie ignored me and barreled ahead. Before I knew it, we were through the lobby and into the hallway on the other side. I am pretty sure we were moving too fast for Amber to recognize me. We probably looked like streaks of light. A moment later, we were at the second exit. When I shoved open the door, there was Yasmeen.

"What took you—?" she started to say. But Luau interrupted with a fierce yowl. When I looked down, I saw the bag was half unzipped and his head was sticking out of it.

"He didn't like not being able to see," Yasmeen explained.

"Where are we going?" Sofie asked me. "What room?"

I told her, and then realized we had to go through the lobby to reach the elevators, which meant there had been no point sneaking Luau in in the first place. I explained this, but Sofie said, "No, we don't," and—it was like a magic trick—she pushed open a door next to the exit and, presto, there was a stairway.

"How did you know stairs would be there?" I asked.

"My family has a lot of money, so we stay in a lot of hotels," Sofie said.

At the door to Room 245, I handed Sofie the plastic card. She was the one with the most experience. She inserted it, a tiny green light on the door blinked, and she turned the knob. "Ready?"

Chapter Fourteen

I don't know why, but Yasmeen and I both walked into the hotel room on tiptoes, and when Yasmeen spoke, it was in a whisper. "We have to hurry!" She unzipped Luau's bag, and he sprang like a jack-in-the-box set free. "Find the recipe!" Yasmeen told him.

"Why are you whispering?" Sofie said in her normal, loud voice. "What recipe? What are we investigating, anyway?"

Luau sat down and washed his face. I looked around. I had never seen a hotel room this big. It was like a fancy apartment, with two bedrooms and even a little living room place. It smelled good, like flowery perfume. And it was perfectly neat and tidy.

"*Alex,* talk to your cat!" Yasmeen looked at her watch. "The volleyball game started at three. It took us longer than we thought to get in here. We have to hurry!"

Luau switched paws to wash the other side of his face. He did not seem to get the purpose of his assignment at all, or to care if we got caught. I knelt next to him.

"Kitty," I said, "somewhere nearby is a recipe that smells like fishy crackers. Your job is to find it."

Luau stretched a long, relaxed stretch. *You zipped me up in the dark and now you're expecting a favor? I think not.*

Sofie doesn't understand cat, but even she could tell that Luau wasn't going anywhere. "Find the recipe," she told him, "and I'll personally see to it you get a lifetime supply of those disgusting smelly crackers."

I could tell Luau liked the sound of "disgusting" and "smelly." He looked at me and blinked, which meant, *well, if you put it* that *way. . . .* Then, still in no hurry, he sniffed the air, looked both ways, and trotted off toward the bedroom on the right.

Sofie plopped down on the sofa.

"Don't touch anything!" Yasmeen and I said at the same time.

Sofie rolled her eyes. "It's not like my posterior is going to leave fingerprints! So . . . do you guys want to tell me what's going on or what?"

There didn't seem to be any reason not to tell her, so Yasmeen did. Meanwhile, I could hear Luau thumping in the other room.

After a minute, Sofie got up off the sofa. "We should look for the recipe, too—open drawers, crawl under the beds, see what's in the bathroom. Maybe we'll find it before Luau does."

"But that would be snooping!" Yasmeen said.

"Earth to Yasmeen," Sofie said. "Snooping is what detectives do."

Sofie was heading for the closet when two things happened at the same time: Luau meowed a surprised and happy meow; someone knocked at the door.

"Hide!" I said.

Yasmeen and I ducked behind the sofa. Sofie didn't. "If whoever it is had a key, they wouldn't knock, they'd just walk in."

It was right as she said "just walk in" that the door opened. A voice in the hall said, "Thank you," and another one said, "Okay." Then the first voice said, "I knew you kids were up to something," and Mrs. Sikora came in and closed the door behind her. "That ridiculous story about animal science classes, Alex. What do you think, I'm dumb or something?"

So much for Sofie's claim that her mom was fooled.

"How did you get in here?" Sofie asked. "You shouldn't be in here. It's private property."

"The maid let me in," Mrs. Sikora said. "I told her it was a life-or-death situation, which it is, because when we get home, I am going to strangle you! What do you think you're doing, sneaking in here?"

"I could ask you that, too, Mom. Just wait till Detective Parakeet finds out about this! You'll probably go to jail!"

There is an old football saying that the best defense is a good offense. This is totally something Sofie believes. She was on her feet, leaning forward, her face pink, her voice raspy. Yasmeen and I, meanwhile, were silent as stones.

The door from the hallway opened again. "Is everything all right in here? Who are *you*?" This time it was Amber.

"Thank goodness. Reinforcements," Mrs. Sikora said. "These kids have a cat in here. That's not allowed, is it?"

Amber said, "Not strictly. But like I said before, who are *you*?"

Mrs. Sikora hesitated, which gave Sofie time to speak. "*We* are friends of Mrs. Parakeet's grandson, Alex Parakeet. But I have no idea who this lady is. We've never seen her before in our lives. It's a tragic thing when children aren't safe from strangers in hotel rooms. Don't you think so?"

Meow? said Luau from the next room.

"Excuse me," I said politely. "I have to check on something."

I scooted into the bedroom, where Luau was sitting on top of a chest of drawers. For a second, I forgot all about Mrs. Sikora and Amber. Was the recipe in one of those drawers?

Luau blinked at me, *Took you long enough.*

I could hear Sofie and her mom arguing. Quickly,

I crossed to the chest, opened the top drawer, and encountered my worst nightmare of what might happen to a snoopy kid—a lady's frilly underwear. Thanks a lot, kitty. I slammed that drawer and tried the next one and then the next one. Clothes and more clothes. It wouldn't be long till someone came in and yanked Luau and me out of here. At least if I found the recipe first, I wouldn't mind so much being grounded for the rest of my life.

Only the bottom drawer to go. I pulled it open, and . . .

. . . the Cheesy Dean jackpot!

Instantly, Luau dropped like a stone from the top of the dresser into a pile of blue and orange bags. *Pop! Pop! Pop!* Three exploded under his weight. Cheesy Deans flew everywhere, and a smell only a cat could love flooded the room. Knowing he had no time for leisurely dining, Luau gulped one fishy cracker whole, clasped another in his teeth, jumped out of the drawer, and tried to slither under the bed.

Too bad for Luau, there was no "under the bed." The mattress was on a platform that blocked off the space beneath. Poor Luau looked so clumsy and frantic nosing around that I started to laugh.

"I don't see anything funny, young man," said a voice from the doorway.

I knew who it was without turning. "Hi, Mom."

Chapter Fifteen

Sofie's best-defense-is-a-good-offense idea had worked pretty well with her own mom. I decided to test it out on mine. "What are you doing here?" I wanted my voice to rasp like Sofie's, but it squeaked instead.

"Amber the desk clerk called 911 to report a disturbance. When she mentioned a cat, I knew who I'd find. So, my son, what exactly is the deal?"

Sofie would never answer directly. She would ask another question to confuse things. But I couldn't think of another question. That's the problem with being basically an honest person. In the end, you always give up and tell the truth: "We were trying to get Dad's recipe back."

"In Zooey and your grandmother's hotel room?"

Without intending to, I wound up telling her exactly what was going on, short version. "We didn't know what else to do, Mom. Dad's desperate. And Zooey Bonjour was our best suspect."

Mom had a funny expression on her face. I thought maybe it meant she was feeling more sympathetic. After all, weren't we just trying to help Dad? But then she pinched her nose, and I realized she was only reacting to the Cheesy Deans. "Come on, kitty." She grabbed Luau by the scruff of his neck and threw him over her shoulder. "*Phew*! Your breath is terrible!"

I followed them back to the living room. Yasmeen, Mrs. Sikora, and Sofie were all sitting on the sofa.

Sofie piped up, "Amber went downstairs because you're here to be in charge now, Detective Parakeet. She said she'll be happy to testify against the burglar. She meant my mom when she said 'burglar.' Are you going to throw my mom in jail? Because if you are, she needs to go to the grocery store first for frozen microwave pizzas. Without frozen microwave pizzas, Byron and me will starve."

Before Mrs. Sikora could speak, the door from the hallway opened and an entire party's worth of people bubbled in. At first, they were having such a good time, they didn't notice that the room was already kind of full up, but after a few seconds, they stopped and looked around.

"Why, Noreen—what are you doing here?" It was Zooey Bonjour. The other people were my grandma, Mr. Stone, and . . . *Bub?*

Already this had been a surprising afternoon. But

this was the biggest surprise yet: What was Bub doing here? And *what had happened to him?*

I have known Bub practically my whole life and I have never seen him wearing anything but sweats or overalls except for once at a Halloween party, when he was wearing bright red long johns. Today he was totally transformed—khaki pants, a white shirt with a collar, and a blue jacket with shiny gold buttons. His usually fluffed-up hair had been combed into submission. His face looked shiny and healthy. I guessed he must've shaved.

Bub could see we were staring, and he grinned. "I clean up nice, don't I?"

Meanwhile, Zooey's question hung in the air. "Noreen?" she repeated.

Grandma chimed in. "I told Alex he could come over to watch the football show on the wide-screen TV. I didn't know he was bringing guests."

Mom looked at me.

"I'll explain the whole thing, Mom, uh . . . later. Because now, you know, it's a school night, and I have a *lot* of homework, and—"

"Me, too!" said Sofie. "How 'bout giving us a ride home, Detective Parakeet? I've always wanted to ride in a police car. Can you turn on the siren, too? I mean, unless you need the car to transport my mom to jail and everything."

"Noreen?" Zooey Bonjour was beginning to sound impatient.

I knew my mom would never lie. But maybe this wasn't a great time to tell the whole truth, either. "The kids were looking for something," my mom said carefully. "And they thought it might be here. Sofie's mom didn't like the idea of their being in your room by themselves, so she came up to help."

"Why did they need Luau?" Grandma asked.

Luau wiped his paw over his eye. *It's nice to be noticed.*

Zooey made a face. "And I believe he has found my Cheesy Deans."

"Of course we brought Luau," Sofie said. "We had to. His job was to sniff out the recipe."

Everybody stared. Sofie shrugged. *"What?"* she said. "That *was* his job! I don't see why there has to be some big secret about it. After a while, all the sneaky-snoop gets on my nerves. Zooey Bonjour, did *you* steal the recipe for Grandma's million-dollar pumpkin pie?"

Chapter Sixteen

Without even looking at Yasmeen, I knew we were having the same thought at the same time. Why do we ever bring Sofie when we're investigating? Once because of Sofie we got trapped by a kidnapper in a pitch-black garage. Another time, Luau almost disappeared forever. Now Sofie had gone and blabbed about the recipe, probably wrecking my dad's chances of being on TV and ever finding his métier in food.

Before Mom or I or Yasmeen could interrupt, Sofie had explained it all. Bub, Mr. Stone, and my grandma all looked a little confused, but Zooey Bonjour—being perfect—looked as if she had understood every word.

"Do you mind if I sit down?" she asked. Then she dropped into a chair, closed her eyes for one long blink, opened them again, and said, "Ted, would you like to tell the others what you told me when we met at the party on Saturday—about the Christmas pageant?"

Mr. Stone laughed, which—since we were all so upset—sounded one part crazy and one part hopeful.

Then he squared his shoulders and cleared his

throat. "When I was a very young lad," he began, "I was selected by my teacher, Miss Nugent, to star as the shepherd boy in the Christmas pageant at my school. Some of you will remember that my dad was a minister and an excellent orator. He was particularly pleased that I was chosen to play the part.

"I was so excited! I practiced my lines from morning till night. My mother stayed up all hours sewing my costume. And I don't mind telling you that all the other children—most of whom were playing sheep and donkeys—were filled with envy.

"At last, the big day came. The parents were assembled. My father was in the front row. I marched out onto the stage to deliver my first line, and . . . what do you think happened?"

He paused and looked into each of our faces, building suspense.

Then he said, "I *froze!*"

"You mean, you couldn't say your lines?" Sofie asked.

"Not only could I not say my lines, Miss Sikora, I could not move! Miss Nugent had to come out from the wings, take my elbow, and usher me offstage. One of the girls—Barbara, I think her name was—took off her lamb's tail and stepped in to play the shepherd boy. She had heard my lines so many times, she knew them by heart."

There was a pause, and then Sofie said what I was thinking: "Is that it? Because it's a really good story, but I have no idea what the point is."

Mr. Stone said, "Then let me add one thing more. While I have no problem telling stories in a small group like this, that was the last time I ever appeared on a stage or ever hope to do so. As I told Ms. Bonjour when she so generously suggested I might share my hot chocolate recipe with her viewers someday, my idea of torture would be appearing on television."

"So then why did you bring hot chocolate to Alex's mom's party?" Sofie Sikora wanted to know.

"It was a gift," he said.

"You mean, like you didn't want anything back from it?" Sofie shook her head. "Weird."

Yasmeen sighed like the air had gone out of her. Here she had this great theory, and it had all come apart. I knew she was embarrassed, but she also had a question, and her curiosity beat out her embarrassment. "There's one other thing," she said. "Last night when we were filing the notes from the neighbors, we found a page from a letter. From what it said, it looked like it was written by somebody you had asked to be on your show this week—somebody who makes your chicken paprika."

Zooey looked surprised. "I can't think how that

got in there—unless it was when I emptied my briefcase . . . ? But it doesn't matter. It has nothing to do with the missing recipe. And beyond that, I'm afraid I can't discuss it."

Yasmeen looked at me. "We're back where we started," she said.

"Well, not quite," Mom said. "Because now you're also in a whole lot of trouble."

Only one thing kept Mom from grounding me that night—and from calling the Popps to make sure Yasmeen was grounded, too. That thing was Toby Lee. By the time we got home from the Knightly Tiger Inn, Mr. Lee had already called Dad twice to ask how soon Yasmeen and I were coming over.

"It's not fair to punish Michael Lee for your transgressions," Mom said. Then she made me promise not to tell Dad about what had happened at the inn that day. He had enough to worry about already, she said.

You wouldn't think pumpkin pie would ever get old, would you? But when Dad handed me a piece at dinnertime, my stomach did an unhappy little flip-flop. I managed to eat it, though—with lots of vanilla ice cream to disguise the taste.

I was putting on my coat when Dad handed me yet another pie to take over to the Lees. He had already sampled it and decided it wasn't right, but he said it did taste pretty good. It featured mashed banana.

Outside, the air wasn't as cold as I'd expected. The TV news had been talking about a blizzard, but maybe it was going some other direction? Mr. Lee would be glad to hear that. Mrs. Lee was supposed to be flying back tomorrow, and when the weather's bad, sometimes they close the airport.

Yasmeen's family lives on the left side of us, and the Lees live on the right. Yasmeen met me coming down the sidewalk, and together we walked over.

"If it wasn't from Mr. Stone, then who was that letter from?" Yasmeen asked, like there hadn't been any break between this afternoon and now. "I don't get it."

"Me, neither. But it doesn't have anything to do with the recipe—Zooey said so."

"How do we know we can trust her?"

"Investigating Zooey only got us into trouble," I said. "Let's investigate somebody else for a change."

Yasmeen looked disgusted. "We can't just pick who we investigate based on what's easiest. We have to base it on *facts*. Do you still have that letter?"

"Yeah, I guess. Grandma hasn't picked up the file box yet. It's probably still where we left it."

There was a pause while the gears spun in Yasmeen's head. Then she said, "I have an idea."

By now, we were standing on the Lees' doorstep. We rang the bell and waited, then rang the bell again. Finally, the door swung open and Mr. Lee—propelled by unseen forces—flew out onto the stoop. I grabbed an elbow, Yasmeen got a shoulder, and together we saved him from tumbling down the steps.

"*Toby!*" Mr. Lee pivoted and flung himself back into the house. "Come on in, guys!" he called to us.

Inside, the living room looked as though a bulldozer had come for a visit. Toys were everywhere, and two plants were flipped over.

I looked around. "Where'd Mr. Lee disappear to?"

"Listen," Yasmeen said. Thumps and bumps were coming from upstairs. "I bet that there's a vacuum cleaner in the hall closet," she went on. "I'll get it. You pick up the toys."

I set down the pie. Yasmeen found the vacuum. When Mr. Lee came down the stairs a few minutes later, the living room looked tidy. He had Toby by the hand, and Baby Alex—bink in her mouth—over his shoulder. Toby was arguing that he wanted to "p'ay 'pooter" in Daddy's office, and Baby Alex was zonked out. There was a wet spot on Mr. Lee's shoulder: baby drool.

"Good to see you guys." Mr. Lee let go of Toby and shook each of our hands, then checked out the living room. "Something's different."

"We cleaned up," Yasmeen said.

Mr. Lee nodded. "No point in that. The toddler tornado will have it back to chaos"—he snapped his fingers—"like that."

On cue, Toby built up a head of steam, careened toward me, and jumped—expecting me to catch him. Unfortunately, I had picked up the pie again. Trying to juggle it to my other hand, I missed—and it crashed to the floor. Toby didn't care. He grabbed my shoulders and clung like a chimpanzee.

Mr. Lee looked down at the broken bits of pie and pie plate.

"Pumpkin?" he said after a moment.

"Yeah," I said.

"My favorite," he said.

"I'll get the broom and dustpan," Yasmeen said.

"Piggyback!" Toby commanded me. *"Piggyback now!"*

With the baby still in his arms, Mr. Lee dropped into a chair, leaned back, and closed his eyes. He was so still that for a minute I thought he was asleep, but then he spoke: "Crossword puzzles? Is that what you needed?"

Yasmeen finished cleaning up and sat down on the sofa to explain.

Doing piggyback laps around the downstairs—living room, dining room, kitchen—I heard pieces of their conversation.

"... symmetrical grid ..."

"... clues can be straight, which means ..."

"... checking letters with the opposite clue ..."

"... big fad in the 1920s ..."

"Giddyap!" Toby kicked to make me go faster.

"Ow!" I said. "I won't go at all if you hurt me."

"Woo-woo-woo-woo-woo!" Toby sang a war cry.

While I kept galloping, Yasmeen kept talking, and everything was fine until Toby leaned down and grabbed the binky from his sister's mouth the way you grab the ring on a merry-go-round. I didn't realize what had happened till Baby Alex started to wail. Mr. Lee handed her to Yasmeen and gave chase. When he caught up to Toby and me, Toby held out his empty hands and said, "No binky."

Baby Alex was still wailing. "Don't you have a spare?" Yasmeen called.

"That *was* the spare! The *spare* spare! Toby has stolen every last one of them. You'd think he enjoys the sound of his sister crying!"

Toby kept grinning.

"Toby, whadidja do with it?" I asked.

Toby showed his empty hands. "Aw gone," he said.

I stopped in my tracks. "Horsey won't go until you give it back."

To my surprise, this actually worked. Toby pointed

me to the kitchen and showed me where the binky was. I'll say this for the kid, he had some arm. He had managed to throw it straight into the garbage disposal. Mr. Lee never would've found it till he turned on the switch and chewed it up.

Yasmeen didn't have any more questions for Mr. Lee. It seemed kind of heartless for us to leave him alone with those kids again, but it was late, and he insisted he could handle it.

Outside, I asked Yasmeen if he had said anything helpful.

"A person who builds crossword puzzles is called a 'cruciverbalist,'" Yasmeen said. "And there was a big craze for them in the twenties."

"My great-grandma would have been around then," I said. "Anything else?"

"Not really about crosswords. But I did find out who bought your grandma's million-dollar pumpkin pie at the auction last year."

"You're kidding! How did Mr. Lee know that?"

"He was bidding on it, too," Yasmeen said. "Pumpkin pie's his favorite, right? But it got too expensive."

"So who bought it?"

"Micah Levin's mom. Micah's in first grade, and he's a friend of Jeremiah's."

"Do they live close? We could go over there," I said.

"Maybe they remember what the pie tasted like. If we find out the secret ingredient, then it doesn't really matter who stole the recipe, does it?"

Yasmeen said of course it mattered. It was important that the bad guy be exposed and punished. I disagreed but it was too cold to argue.

We decided to go to the Levins' house after school. They lived over on Robin Road, not that far, and Jeremiah would love to come with us and see Micah.

"I have another idea," Yasmeen said.

My teeth were chattering. "How about if I hear it in the morning, when the sun's out?"

"Handwriting," Yasmeen said, ignoring my answer, as usual. "We take that letter around looking for a match for the handwriting. If we find one, then we know who's conspiring with Zooey Bonjour to replace your dad on the show!"

Chapter Seventeen

Except for the porch light, the house was dark when I got home. So I wouldn't forget, I took the mystery letter out of the file box in the hall first. Then I called a quick good-night to my parents and went to bed.

I couldn't fall asleep at first. I was worrying about how Zooey Bonjour was mad at us. Plus we still hadn't found the recipe. When I finally dropped off, all kinds of two-word mystery ingredients were projected on the back of my eyelids: Diet Coke, feta cheese, scrambled eggs, cough syrup.

It didn't help that Luau was having a restless night, too. And, *sheesh*, did his breath smell terrible!

When the alarm went off, I shoved him away. "Next time you eat Cheesy Deans, you're sleeping with Mom and Dad."

Luau *mrrf*ed and yawned: *You don't smell like a bouquet of posies yourself, you know.*

Being sleepy made me slow getting ready for school, but that turned out to be lucky, because there was no time to eat the pumpkin pie Dad offered me for breakfast; I grabbed a granola bar instead. Out on the sidewalk with Yasmeen, I said, "Weren't we just here?"

"You were yawning then, too. Hey, look—it's Bub and Officer Krichels!"

Bub and his buddy were jogging toward us and smiling. Smiling at 7:40 in the morning! That just proves you have to be crazy to exercise before breakfast! Bub looked normal again. He was wearing his old gray sweats, and he hadn't shaved. Officer Krichels was dressed in regular running clothes. He looked like a yardstick with a nose.

"Hey, you kids—good morning!" Officer Krichels called. The two of them passed us on the sidewalk, then made a U-Turn so they could jog alongside us while we walked to the corner.

"I missed saying good-bye to you two yesterday afternoon," Bub said. "Detective Parakeet sure hustled you out pronto."

Yasmeen said, "Yeah, Bub, we didn't get a chance to ask. What were you even doing there?"

Bub explained that Mr. Stone had asked him to go along and keep my grandma company, which prompted Officer Krichels to chant: "Bub and Grandma sittin' in a tree, k-i-s-s-i-n-*g*!"

Bub snorted. "Aw, quit your joshin'. An accomplished, professional woman like her would never be interested in a washed-up ol' coalcracker like me."

"I dunno, Bub," Yasmeen said. "You looked pretty handsome yesterday."

"Well, there, you got a point," Bub agreed. "Because by the end of the evening, I'd gone and gotten myself a position as an EAT network understudy. If it turns out your dad can't go on Saturday, Alex, your grandma asked me to take his place—me and my minestrone, that is."

I couldn't believe it! We'd been worrying about Mrs. Aaron and Mr. Stone, but all the time the threat was . . . Bub!

I guess my reaction showed on my face because Bub was quick to reassure me. "Now, it's *only* if the recipe doesn't turn up, Alex. Zooey and your grandma are still hoping it will, and so am I. But they gotta have a backup plan, after all. It's live television!"

By now, we were at the corner, with the school bus rumbling toward us.

"Come on, Fred." Bub signaled. "Once more around Mailbox Park. You kids, you have a good day at school now!"

The bus wheezed to a stop, and the doors squeaked opened. Yasmeen and I took our regular seats four rows back on the right. I was tired and grumpy and ready to whine, but Yasmeen, as usual, wouldn't listen.

"We can do what you suggested and go over to

Micah's this afternoon," she said. "Then, after that, we take the letter and compare handwriting."

"Take the letter where?" I asked.

"Aaron Farm, to start with," Yasmeen said.

"We don't have to go all the way out there. Mrs. Aaron's coming to Thanksgiving, remember?"

"That's right!" Yasmeen said. "And if Mrs. Aaron's writing isn't a match, we can check out other people's, too—Bub's, for example. I mean, think about it, Alex. Just about everybody coming to your house tomorrow is a potential suspect!"

It was times like this when (a) I wasn't so sure I liked detecting, and (b) I wasn't so sure I liked Yasmeen. To her, solving the case was all about puzzles and justice. To me, it was all about work and getting somebody in trouble.

Yasmeen and I usually don't sit together on the bus home. We don't always get out of class at the same time, and then there's the harassment factor. Twice, people have asked if she's my *girlfriend*, even though they know she's totally not. That day after school, I sat with Ari. He's the one with the cocker spaniel, plus he was on my baseball team last summer. Ari's family was leaving right away to drive to New York City to see relatives, he said. His dad was worried about the weather forecast, though.

I looked out the window. "There's only a little snow on the road."

"Yeah, but everybody says it's supposed to get worse."

After Ari's stop is Yasmeen's and mine. When the doors opened, snowflakes blew in. "Happy Thanksgiving!" I said to Mr. Wilson, the bus driver.

"You, too, Alex. Bye-bye there, Yasmeen!"

As soon as I walked in the front door of my house, I realized something was funny. But what? Oh yeah! For the first time in days, it didn't smell like pumpkin pie!

In the kitchen, I explained to dad that it was Mrs. Levin who bought the million-dollar pie last year. "Is it okay for Yasmeen and me to go over to where they live on Robin Road?" I asked. "Maybe they remember the taste well enough to identify the secret ingredient."

Dad said it was worth a try and told me to be careful on the slippery sidewalks.

A couple of minutes later, Yasmeen arrived with Jeremiah. She was carrying a plastic bag, and inside was a very small present. "Jeremiah says they've got a new baby," Yasmeen said. "So my mom told me to take this."

The walk to Robin Road from my house goes past St. Bernard's Church and Mailbox Park, then around the corner by our old elementary school. A couple of times we could hardly see, the snow was blowing so hard. I couldn't help thinking that a Thanksgiving storm is rotten luck. You don't even get a snow day out of it.

Like most houses in College Springs, the Levins' had a Knightly Tiger flag flying. Jeremiah rang the bell, and a little kid pulled the door open so fast, he must have been on the other side waiting for us.

"Micah!"

"Jeremiah!"

They tumbled on top of each other.

"Hello, hello . . . welcome!" A pretty woman with dark hair wearing Knightly Tiger sweatpants and a black T-shirt came into the front hall. She had a bundle in her arms, which she handed off to Yasmeen like it was a bag of flour. Then she turned to help Jeremiah with his boots and coat. The bundle, meanwhile, turned out to be a baby, which luckily Yasmeen knows about, because Jeremiah used to be one.

Mrs. Levin stood up, took the baby back, and smiled at us. "Now, you two can get your things off and then come sit down for a bit. Around here it's 'Jeremiah says this,' and 'Jeremiah says that.' I guess that little brother of yours is quite a bright one, Yasmeen."

"What's the baby's name?" Yasmeen asked.

"Giacomo—Jack, for short," she said.

"Like Coach Patronelli," I said.

Mrs. Levin smiled. "Right you are. Coach Patronelli's my dad—or did you know that?"

"*Oh!*" Yasmeen and I said at the same time. Then I remembered. The other day at Mailbox Park, he had said he was visiting his new grandson on Robin Road.

"And this Jack's a little football fan, too," Mrs. Levin was saying. "When the game's on, he sits in his bouncy chair and watches. I think he's studying the I-formation."

We settled in at the kitchen table. "Does Micah like football?" I asked.

"Takes it or leaves it." Mrs. Levin filled the kettle and put it on the stove. "But he likes the tailgate parties— especially the Tiger Band when they march through."

Mrs. Levin offered us a plate of cookies, then sat down herself.

"I almost forgot—we brought you a present!" Yasmeen said.

Mrs. Levin made the usual "Oh, you didn't have to!" noises, then tore off the paper as happily as a kid. Inside was a pair of tiny jewel earrings, and Yasmeen explained that her mom always gives tiny earrings to new moms because babies can't grab them the way they do big earrings.

Mrs. Levin thanked us both, even though I had nothing to do with it. Then we ate cookies and drank tea with sugar and talked about the big game against Ohio on Saturday. I was hoping Mrs. Levin would give away some secrets about the team's preparations, but before she had the chance there was a series of loud bangs followed by Jeremiah chasing Micah into the kitchen.

"Samich! Samich! Samich!" Micah chanted.

Mrs. Levin sighed and got up. "What kind of jelly do you like, Jeremiah?"

Micah and Jeremiah answered together: "Strawberry!"

Mrs. Levin took a jar of peanut butter as big as a football from the cupboard and said, "This one's almost done. I'll have to go out on Friday. If we don't have plenty for the tailgate, Micah will starve."

Yasmeen turned to Jeremiah. "We should go home when you're done with your sandwich," she said. "Alex and I both have to help with Thanksgiving."

"I can't wait till these guys are old enough to help me," Mrs. Levin said. "Last year, I didn't have to make dessert, at least. We had that wonderful pie from the school auction. It was a huge hit—especially with my dad."

"Alex's father made that pie," Yasmeen said. "That's one reason we came over."

While Mrs. Levin served the sandwiches and milk, I told her about the pie and the missing recipe and said we hadn't even realized that her family had bought last year's pie till yesterday. "Yasmeen and I never got to try it," I said. "So we were hoping you'd remember something that might help us identify the secret ingredient. Can you describe what it tasted like?"

"It just had a special quality," Mrs. Levin said. "More—what's the word I want?—*character* than your average pumpkin pie."

"Did its character taste like anything in particular?" Yasmeen asked.

Mrs. Levin shrugged. "Extreme pumpkin? Oh, you guys, I'm sorry I'm no help. And I'm *really* sorry there's not going to be another one of those pies this year! Even Micah was enthused, and he's very picky."

When Jeremiah was done with his sandwich, there was the regular zipping of coats and tugging of hats and mittens and snow boots. Then, with Baby Jack in her arms and Micah beside her, Mrs. Levin stood at the front door and waved good-bye to us.

The sidewalks had about an inch of snow on them by now, and the wind was fierce. When I opened the front door at my house, my eyes were watering, my teeth were chattering, and there was a snot icicle on the tip of my nose.

Chapter Eighteen

On Thanksgiving morning, Luau woke me with a high-pitched *mrrrow* that meant, *Look outside!*

I raised myself on my elbows and looked through the frosty window to see that snow had transformed everything—bushes, fences, rooftops, and cars—into soft marshmallow blobs. It was still coming down, too.

I looked at the clock. Eight A.M. For now, it was absolutely quiet outside, like no one even lived on our street. Later, you could bet that kids would go out and make snowmen, grown-ups would clear the walks, and someone my mom would label "crazy fool" would dig a car out and try to drive away. But for now the neighbors were just like me and Luau, inside looking out at the snow as if snow had never happened before.

In the bathroom, I got ready to face the day: I brushed, I washed, I brushed. And I thought about Grandma's million-dollar pumpkin pie. With Zooey's show on Saturday, Yasmeen and I were running out of time, and so far every one of our ideas had been a dead end. I didn't want the bad guy to be Mrs. Aaron, but I still hoped Yasmeen's plan to match up handwriting worked.

I have learned there are two kinds of families in America: families who eat Thanksgiving dinner at dinnertime, and families who eat Thanksgiving dinner early. We are early eaters. My dad says that's so there's plenty of time before you go to bed to clean up and digest. But really it's so there's plenty of time before you go to bed to fix a whole second dinner of leftovers.

It was 8:15 A.M. when I got downstairs, and Thanksgiving Preps, Day II, were in full swing. Underneath their aprons, my parents were already dressed up and ready for company.

"What's for breakfast?" I asked.

Dad and Mom both looked at me and scowled.

I nodded. "Right. I'll be making my own breakfast."

Luau, who had followed me downstairs, side-rubbed my legs. I told him to make his own breakfast, too. He went directly to the cupboard that held the bags of Cheesy Deans.

Meow? he asked politely.

I shook my head no. "I can't take any more of that sardine breath!" Then I poured him a bowl of his regular cat food. He sat down. Then he looked at the food and looked at me: *I'll eat it. But don't expect me to thank you for it.*

I got myself cereal and cleared a place at the table. Then I had a terrible thought. "We're not having pumpkin pie for dessert, are we?" I asked.

"No way!" Mom said.

Dad smiled. "I don't think I could choke down another bite of pumpkin," he said. "Zooey Bonjour is bringing dessert. I'm sure it will be something special!"

My bowl of cereal was empty, so it was time to be a good family citizen and volunteer for the least horrible job. "Do you want me to set the table?"

"Oh, honey, that would be *great*!" Mom said.

"So how many people are coming?"

Dad had been bending over the oven, basting the turkey, while Luau sat patiently and watched—ready to pounce if the turkey jumped up and made a run for it. Now Dad closed the oven door, straightened up, and counted on his fingers. When he had used all ten of his, he grabbed Mom's hand and kissed it—*Yuck*—then counted hers.

"Fourteen," he said finally, "including Officer Krichels. But to tell the truth, this weather has me worried. The airport's closed—I heard it on the radio. And with the roads so bad, I bet some people who were planning to leave are stranded."

"Like Ari's family," I said. "They were supposed to

drive to New York, but his dad was worried about the weather."

Dad and Mom looked at each other.

"We've got plenty of food," Dad said.

"I'm not sure about silverware," Mom said.

"Don't we have my grandmother's in the basement?" Dad asked.

"That's right!" Mom said. "I bet it's a sight, but we can clean it up. Honey," Mom turned to me, "why don't you call Ari's family? If they're still here, tell them we'd be happy to include them."

I put my cereal bowl in the dishwasher and called Ari's house. A few minutes later, I reported back to my mom and dad. "Ari's mom was really grateful. They were thinking they'd have to eat turkey hot pockets."

Dad shuddered. "Who buys those awful things?"

Mom looked at Dad and laughed. "You are like a nutrition fiend lately!"

Nutrition made me think of Marjie Lee. Hadn't she gone to a family nutrition school? "Did you say the airport's closed?" I asked. "Because Marjie Lee was supposed to fly back last night."

Being a cop, Mom recognizes an emergency when she sees one. "*Oh, no.* You mean Michael Lee is still stuck over there by himself with those kids?" In a flash, she had slipped off her apron and gone to get her snow boots. "I'll go check on them. And we'll need two more places for dinner, Alex, plus the high chair."

"It's in the basement with the silver," Dad said. "And that should be on the shelves by the furnace." He handed me a rag. "It'll be dusty."

Dad's grandma's silver chest was under two boxes of Christmas ornaments and three fluorescent light tubes. Coughing, I did my best with the rag to clean off the cobwebs and corpses of spiders and bugs. Then I carried the chest upstairs and opened it at the kitchen table. The brown velvet inside was surprisingly clean, and the silver still glowed, although some of it had yellowy brown spots.

Dad looked over my shoulder. "There's time if you want to polish it before you wash it. It's kind of fun to get it gleaming again."

Fun. *Right.*

Dad brought out the silver polish, which reminded me of toothpaste in a can, and I rubbed down the forks, knives, and spoons. The yellowy brown stuff disappeared fast. As jobs go, polishing is not as good as taste-testing frosting or even twisting crepe paper, but it's not as bad as I expected.

I was almost done when I noticed a brittle piece of paper poking out from between the velvet lining and the wooden box. Curious, I tugged a corner of the velvet, and discovered that the lining lifted out. The paper underneath turned out to be a page from a newspaper dated Sunday, November 23, 1924. On it were recipes, all for Thanksgiving.

Dad was washing pots at the sink. The water was running, so I had to shout. "Hey, Dad—what grandma did this silverware belong to, anyway?"

"Grandma Bea, my father's mother. Why?"

"'Cause look at this." I got up and showed him the newspaper.

Dad smiled. "That's a piece of family history right there," he said. "Look—that's the recipe for yam-and-cornbread stuffing that I still use."

Dad and I looked at each other—same thought, same moment. Was it possible Grandma's pumpkin pie recipe was right here in front of our eyes?

Together, we read the recipe titles aloud: "Green beans with onion and sausage, creamy turkey pan gravy, whipped potatoes, flaky buttermilk biscuits, pumpkin pie. . . ."

Pumpkin pie?

I whooped and started my touchdown dance, but Dad interrupted with a hand on my shoulder. "Wait a sec, bud. We gotta calm down and check this out."

He took the paper and read off the ingredients: pie

shell, pumpkin, heavy cream, brown sugar, granulated sugar, salt, cinnamon, ground ginger, nutmeg, ground cloves, eggs.

Then he sighed and sagged back against the counter. "That's Thanksgiving pie, all right. Except something's missing."

"The secret ingredient," I said.

"Oh, well." He shook himself back to life. "Easy come, easy go. Plus," he looked down at the paper, "this looks like a good gravy recipe. I just might use it today."

Usually, I think my mom is the tough one in the family—the cop. But today Dad was acting tough, too. He had to be super-disappointed about this whole pie thing, but he shook it off and got back to work. Me? I wanted to cry. I at least wanted to call Yasmeen. But I had silver to wash and dry, the table to set, and the potatoes to mash. . . .

Dad took the paper and placed it so he could see the gravy recipe. I went to the sink and washed off Great-grandma Bea's silverware. It looked pretty shiny, if I do say so myself. After I dried it, I went into the dining room and looked at the table. Because we were having so much company this year, Dad had extended our regular dining room table with a card table. It was going to be a tight fit, and we hadn't even added the high chair yet.

I set the table, giving everybody minimum space,

and was just laying out the last salad fork when I heard the front door open. Mom was back.

"Alex? How's the silverware supply?" she called.

Before I could answer, there was some clatter and commotion, and a child's voice hollered, "I wanna p'ay wif da kitty!"

Then there was a quick succession of sounds: Mom saying, "Hold on a sec. Let me get your boots off before you—"; Luau's footpads skedaddling at top speed down the basement stairs; some kind of stomp-and-whine, bump-and-*oof* struggle in the hall; and the pounding of a small person running.

With his snow boots still attached to his feet, Toby Lee plunged into the dining room, leaving a trail of puddles and snow clumps behind him. *"Kitty?"* he squealed, looking right and left. Then he honed in on my knees and hurtled into them, knocking me back against the table and making the glasses clatter.

"What are you doing here?" I asked—not very politely. *"Mom?"*

"I had to bring him." Mom came in. "Marjie Lee is stuck at the airport in D.C. Another minute, and Michael wouldn't have been responsible. . . . Gimme those boots, Toby! Then we'll find the kitty."

"I doubt that," I said. The last time Toby played with Luau, he stuck stick-on ribbons all over his tail. Luau had never been so humiliated—not to mention that it hurt when I pulled the ribbons off. Hearing Toby, my cat had probably gotten himself so lost, he'd never be found.

"You p'omised kitty!" Toby frowned at my mom.

"I would have promised anything." Mom sat down on the floor to pull Toby's boots off while he clung to my knees. He was dressed in a snowy snowsuit and mittens, and by now my jeans were wet with Toby snot and melted snow.

"Silverware?" my mom repeated.

Leg by leg, I escaped Toby's grasp and counted what was left in the chest. "We've got loads," I said.

Mom said good, because she had invited the Sikoras. I looked at the table. "We'll never fit!"

Mom was now being dragged out of the dining room by Toby, who was chanting, "Kitty! Kitty! Kitty!"

"We'll figure something out," she said. "*Ow!* I think he just dislocated my shoulder."

Dad came in through the kitchen door. "Hi, Toby, my man. What's shakin'?" He looked up at Mom. "More guests?"

"No choice," said Mom, still playing tug-of-war. "When I got outside, I saw a tree was down in the Sikoras' yard. I went to make sure they were okay, and Babs told me the tree took their power line out. We can't very well let neighbors have a cold Thanksgiving dinner in the dark."

"We're lucky we haven't lost power," Dad said. "I'd better get out some candles, just in case."

Mom tried to shake Toby loose. "Okay, that's enough, kiddo."

Dad nodded at Toby, who hadn't let go. "I guess I don't have to ask how the Lees are getting along."

"Better without this one, I suspect. . . . Toby? How about cartoons?"

Toby turned and, with no warning, let go of my mom's hand, causing her to lose her balance and fall backward onto the floor. *Ouch.* Toby exploded in giggles and pointed: "Miz Par'keet fell on her—"

From the floor, Mom shot him her patented laser death stare, which—deployed at maximum force—was enough to silence even Toby Lee.

After the table was set, Mom told me the two available chores were minding Toby and shoveling the walk. Rubbing her shoulder, she said she picked the walk. Toby, meanwhile, was grinning and looking around as if he was trying to spot an object that would make lots of noise when it broke.

I still wanted to call Yasmeen, but I was afraid Toby might escape.

One thing I've learned lately: Some chores aren't so bad. And right up there with frosting and streamers is playing Lousy Luigi III with Toby to keep him out of the way. Toby is pretty good at Lousy Luigi, which is lucky, because anytime he loses, he throws the controller at the TV. The company was coming around one o'clock, and at twelve thirty, my dad came into the family room. He had taken his apron off.

"Go up and change, Alex. I'll take care of this character. Bet I can beat you, Tobe-meister."

"No way!" Toby said.

"Whaddaya mean, change?" I said.

Dad took the controller from me and said, "Your clothes?"

I thought I looked good. My socks were clean.

"Put on the button-down shirt and corduroys you got for your birthday. Don't forget to take the tags off. And fix your hair!"

Upstairs, I found the pants and shirt in my closet. They fit, but they were scratchy. In the bathroom, I splashed water on my hair and smashed it flat. From downstairs came the sounds of people arriving—the doorbell, stomping in the front hall, laughing, and talking.

Even though I had to put on scratchy new clothes . . . even though we hadn't found the recipe . . . even though I would have to put up with Toby Lee and Sofie Sikora all afternoon, I still love Thanksgiving.

Chapter Nineteen

The doorbell kept ringing. The house filled with people, and the front hall, with coats and boots and hats and mittens. There was lots of noise and laughing because everybody was in a happy mood—everybody except Mr. Lee, that is. Not that Mr. Lee was grumpy. Grumpy takes energy. Slumped on the sofa in the living room, he stared out through glassy eyes. In his lap was Baby Alex, alert and sucking on a fresh bink like it was a lollipop.

Yasmeen was in the living room, too, talking to Sofie Sikora. That was a surprise. After Tuesday, I didn't think either of us was ever going to speak to Sofie again, but now she and Yasmeen were acting totally palsy.

"Did you get the mystery letter out of the file box?" Yasmeen asked me.

"Happy Thanksgiving, Yasmeen," I said. "Happy Thanksgiving, Sofie."

"Happy Thanksgiving, Alex," Yasmeen said. "Did you get the mystery letter out of the file box?"

"It's in my room," I said. "So when we get hand-writing samples, we can compare."

"We've already got samples from the people who left recipes for Zooey at your mom's party," Yasmeen said. "But not everybody did. And that's where Sofie comes in. Are you ready, Sofie?"

Sofie shrugged. "Sure. Up there?" She pointed at the raised hearth in front of our fireplace.

"Good as any place," Yasmeen said. "And thanks." Yasmeen had been holding a fat brown envelope, and now she handed it to Sofie. What was going on, anyway?

Sofie stepped up onto the hearth, turned around, and hollered at all the company, "*People? Hello!* We need you to do us a favor, okay?"

I swear Sofie's voice was so loud, it made the house vibrate.

"These are place cards!" Sofie opened the envelope, pulled out a stack of off-white folded-over cards, and held them up. "Alex, Yasmeen, and I are going to hand one to each of you, and you write your own name on it, okay? Then we'll put them at your places at the table, which we're doing so nobody sits in the wrong place at the table. Do you got that, people?"

I had to hand it to Yasmeen. This was smart. We wouldn't have only Mrs. Aaron's handwriting to compare—we would have everybody's!

After Sofie finished talking she handed the envelope to Yasmeen who gave me a handful of cards, took some herself, and gave the rest back to Sofie. "We'll meet in the dining room when we're done," Yasmeen said.

It took me a while to collect names, because everybody wanted to say thank you and chitchat. Ari's dad was really grateful not to be stuck in a snowbank in New Jersey someplace, and Aunt Kate told me three times how handsome I looked. Officer Krichels wanted to know how soon we were going to eat and whether the gravy was the kind with giblets or not. Officer Krichels favored giblets.

In the hall, I came to Zooey Bonjour, Mr. Stone, and Byron Sikora. Byron was saying something to Zooey about how he'd been sick on Monday and had spent the whole day watching her on TV. At first, he was disappointed she didn't have a sword, but when he saw her cut the head off a fish with a big knife, it was almost as good.

I was nervous about seeing Zooey Bonjour after what had happened at the Knightly Tiger Inn. I wouldn't have blamed her if she didn't want to speak to me, or Yasmeen or Sofie, ever again.

But she smiled. "I've made some blunders in my life, too, sweetie. Live and learn, right?"

"I am really sorry," I said.

"Forgiven." She wrote her name neatly and handed the pen to Mr. Stone so he could write his, too.

Bub and Grandma were sitting on the sofa in the family room. He was talking about somebody named James Stewart and how he was from Pennsylvania. Bub was dressed up again—this time wearing gray slacks and a striped shirt, the kind with buttons.

"Who's James Stewart?" I asked.

"You've never heard of Jimmy Stewart?!" my grandma said.

"Did he play for the Steelers?" I asked.

Bub groaned. "Jimmy Stewart was a famous actor from right on over there in Indiana, Pennsylvania. Haven't you ever seen *It's a Wonderful Life*?"

Before I could answer, Grandma said, "Your friend Bub knows more about cinema than almost anyone I've ever met."

"Cinema?" I said.

Bub winked. "She means movies. And in my case, it's all a function of me sittin' on my keister watchin' the TV. I don't deserve any credit for it."

Grandma laughed. "You do yourself a disservice. Anyone can watch a movie, but you have made yourself a student of film."

"Well, shoot and shucks." Bub looked down at his shoelaces and smiled.

I gave Bub and Grandma each a place card, and watched as they wrote down their names. They looked pretty comfortable sitting together on the sofa. But Officer Krichels was only joking with that "k-i-s-s-i-n-g," right?

Those were my last two place cards, so I said thank you and headed for the dining room. Yasmeen was already there. "Take a look at Mrs. Aaron's handwriting," she said, and she handed me the card. Mrs. Aaron's signature featured two big capital letters—J for Jewel and A for Aaron—with the rest smaller and more delicate. "It's possible," I said. "But we need to compare it with the letter, side by side."

"After dinner we'll have time," Yasmeen said.

When Sofie came in, Yasmeen told us, "The guests are supposed to sit boy-girl-boy-girl."

"Who made that rule?" Sofie asked. Yasmeen said, "Etiquette."

"Who invited Etiquette?" I said, which made Sofie laugh and Yasmeen roll her eyes.

By now, it was almost time for dinner. In the kitchen, Dad, Mom, and Aunt Kate were setting out the food in special containers called chafing dishes, which have little flames under them to keep things warm. The old newspaper page I had found in the silver chest was still on the counter. Dad must have used the gravy recipe because there were three brown stains on it. Yasmeen picked up the page and flipped it over.

"Hey," she said, "what's this? A crossword puzzle? Just like—"

But before she could finish the sentence, there was a *whump* from outside.

"Uh-oh," said Jeremiah.

The lights flickered, blazed back, and then went dark altogether, causing the guests to chorus a three-part response: *"Ah!"* (surprise), *"Whew!"* (relief), *"Oh!"* (disappointment).

"Candles!" Mom said. "You got them out, right, Dan?"

"Well, I sure meant to," Dad said. "Bub, can you get a fire going? Mom? Where are you? Can you help?"

"Our power's been out all day," bragged Mrs. Sikora.

"I hope the food doesn't get cold," said Officer Krichels.

"How are we gonna watch football?" whined Uncle Scott.

"Alex!" Mom sent me, Yasmeen, and Ari upstairs to find candles and our camping lantern. Unbelievably, they were on the exact shelf where she said they would be. When we came down, Professor Popp took the lantern to the kitchen, and Zooey Bonjour and Ari's mom distributed candles among the other rooms while Grandma and Mrs. Aaron followed along with matches.

With the candles lit and the fire going, the house turned sparkly and festive.

Soon it was time to eat, and everybody lined up behind Officer Krichels to serve themselves.

On holidays, Dad likes to wait till everybody is sitting down and then say something serious about being all together and grateful and lucky. Knowing there would be a crowd this year, he had even written out a little speech. My family knows the drill, but not all the guests did. Officer Krichels, for one, started to chow down the moment his rear hit the seat cushion—even though Bub kept giving him significant looks and shaking his head. "Got a twitch, there, Bub?" Officer Krichels asked between bites. "Food's sure delicious!"

The way the boy-girl worked out, I was sitting next to Sofie. Nobody was listening, so I said, "Are you still in trouble with your mom?"

"Grounded without possibility of parole," Sofie said. "But it's not like they could keep me from eating Thanksgiving dinner. That would be un-American."

"It's kind of our fault," I said, "Yasmeen's and mine. You wouldn't even have been there, except—"

"I wanted to be there!" Sofie said. "It was fun."

It had taken all this time for Dad to get seated at the head of the table. Now he tapped his knife against his glass to get everybody's attention. "While we're all here together, I'd like to say a few words." He took his speech out of his pocket, then looked around, counting the guests. "Is everyone here?"

They'd better be, I thought. I bumped Ari's mom's elbow every time I inhaled, and the only person with plenty of room was Baby Alex in the high chair. Looking at her, I realized who was missing.

Mom figured it out, too. "Toby, where's your dad?"

Toby was perched on two phone books and a cushion. He had Bub on one side—a violation of the boy-girl etiquette rule—and Mrs. Aaron on the other. She was cutting bites of turkey for him. Toby shrugged. "Doh know."

Mom said, "Alex, could you . . . ?"

Our chairs were crammed together so close that there was only one way out: backward. I bent my knees up under me, put both feet on the seat, pushed up, lifted my right foot, and tried to step over the back. Unfortunately, this unbalanced the chair, which tipped and crashed to the floor. I thought I was toast, but by some miracle, I landed standing up, and the move looked as if I had planned it that way.

Sofie said, "That was *slick!*" Toby instantly tried to copy me, but Bub laid a big hand on his small head.

I found Mr. Lee right away, still in the living room, asleep on the sofa. With the fire, it was cozy, and he looked peaceful. I covered him with an afghan and went back to my dinner. "Mr. Lee can eat later," I reported.

"Might not be anything left," Officer Krichels said. "Anyone for seconds?" I looked at his plate. Not even a cranberry smear.

Dad took his speech out of his pocket again, and tapped his knife against his glass. "While we're all here together, I'd like to say a few—"

Officer Krichels said, "Excuse me," and started the complicated process of getting up from the table. To let him by, Grandma, Bub, Aunt Kate, and Byron Sikora all had to stand up and push their chairs back. This caused a lot of noise, a little grumbling, and one piercing *Ow!* when Byron's toe got trampled.

Dad tried again. "While we're all here together—"

Officer Krichels called from the kitchen, "Is the cat allowed to eat the mashed potatoes?"

"Uh-oh," said Jeremiah.

Mom scrunched her eyes shut the way that meant she was trying not to scream. "Deal with your cat, Alex," she said. "*Please.*"

I could see I was going to get good at the incredible tip-over-chair trick. When I got to the kitchen, Officer Krichels was frowning at the empty potato dish. Luau, no fool, was long gone. "Now's your chance to serve yourself some more, son," Officer Krichels said.

"I had nine brothers and sisters, and I learned the hard way. If you don't get fed early, sometimes you don't get fed."

By the time everybody had been back for seconds, and thirds, I could see Officer Krichels's point. The serving table looked as if piranha had swum through, leaving nothing but turkey bones, a string bean, and two cranberries.

Between dinner and dessert on Thanksgiving, we usually do some cleaning up and watch some football. With the power off, football wasn't happening. So instead, most of the kids played Monopoly by the fire, while the grown-ups and Yasmeen talk-talk-talked. When Mr. Lee woke up, I worried there was no food left for him, but it turned out Zooey Bonjour had set a plate aside.

The power was still out when Zooey called from the kitchen: "Dessert is ready!"

Most everybody headed back to the table, eager to see what fabulous dessert the famous TV chef had made for us. But Mr. Lee, Toby, and Baby Alex stayed in the living room. This time it was Baby Alex who was asleep—napping on Mr. Lee's lap—and he didn't want to disturb her.

Once again, it took a while to get us all seated. Then Zooey came through the kitchen door carrying a platter.

On it were two fat cylinders—like mini fireplace logs, only covered with frosting and sugar and tiny silver sparkly things. They were beautiful. Everybody applauded while Zooey stood smiling and looking proud.

I said, "I'm sure glad it's not pumpkin pie."

Zooey laughed. "I wouldn't want to compete with your dad on that score. But I did want to stay traditional. These are pumpkin rolls—pumpkin cake rolled around pumpkin filling."

Pumpkin?

A groan formed in my throat, but I swallowed it.

Dad had his glasses on. "While we're all here together, I'd like to say a few—"

From the living room came a horrible, *"Waaah!"* And then Mr. Lee's angry, *"Toby!"*

"Uh-oh," said Jeremiah.

Mom looked at me. I performed the tip-over chair trick. Dad crumpled his speech and tossed it in the air. Toby burst into the dining room, laughing like a maniac. There was a pink bink in his fist.

"Catch him!" Mr. Lee called.

I got a hand on him, but he twisted free and nearly crashed into Zooey, who raised the platter over her head and did the cha-cha to stay on her feet.

Toby couldn't get past her to the kitchen. *Now I had him!* I dived. But at the last second he found a hole and squirted through like toothpaste. Instead of tackling Toby, I tackled Zooey.

The pumpkin rolls went flying. Flat on the floor, I closed my eyes and waited for the platter to bounce off my head, but before Jeremiah could even say uh-oh, Yasmeen had lunged across the table and plucked it out of the air.

Save and a beauty! The crowd goes wild!

Hard on Toby's heels, with crying Baby Alex in his arms, Mr. Lee stepped awkwardly over me and Zooey— "Excuse me! Excuse me!"—and ran into the kitchen. Toby's footsteps drummed down the basement stairs.

"Are you all right?" I asked Zooey.

"Never mind *me*," she said. "I spent two days on those pumpkin rolls!"

Dad said, "Only a flesh wound. We can fix it with frosting."

In the end, I was glad for that extra frosting. It disguised the taste of pumpkin. While everyone was eating, we heard the sound of a big truck rumbling down our street, and Mr. Sikora looked out the window. "Electric company," he said, "at last!"

A second later, Mr. Lee came into the dining room, carrying teary-eyed Baby Alex and dragging Toby by the hand. Toby's lips were pressed together.

"Sorry—so sorry for all the commotion," Mr. Lee said loudly so we could hear him over Alex's whimpering. "And now Toby won't tell me where the bink is."

Toby shrugged and said, "Doh know."

Professor Popp said, "With all the detective power in this room, surely someone can find a bink!"

It was like a challenge, and the kids—Ari, Yasmeen, Jeremiah, Sofie, Byron, and I—fanned out to look. Toby had been carrying the bink when he went through the dining room, so it had to be either in the kitchen or in the basement.

We looked everywhere in the kitchen—gravy boat, soup pot, water pitcher. . . . We even looked in the garbage disposal. No bink.

Since the basement was going to be black and scary without lights, Mom gave each of us a candle. As we went down the stairs, I heard Mrs. Popp say we looked like angels in the Christmas Eve service.

It turned out to be fun to hunt around the dark basement with candles—like some kind of haunted pinball game, with us as the pinballs. Soon we were tired, goofy, and breathless. But we still hadn't found Baby Alex's bink.

"I know," Yasmeen said finally. "We need to stop and think like Toby."

"You always think we have to think," I said.

"Well, this time she's right," Ari said. "Toby's a mean, rotten little kid. So how do mean, rotten little kids think?"

"Sofie?" Yasmeen said.

"Mean, rotten kids want to cause the most trouble with the least amount of work," Sofie said. Then she paused. "Hey—why are you asking *me*?"

"Least work makes sense," I said. "He didn't have much time. Toby knew his dad was gonna catch him. Plus it was dark down here."

"So he would've stashed the bink the first place he could," said Ari. "But it wasn't in the kitchen. . . ."

"I know," Yasmeen said. "I will reenact the crime!" She grabbed a jar lid from a shelf, announced, "This is the bink," walked over to the stairs, and climbed them. In the dark, we could follow her progress by the candle's flame. When she reached the top of the stairs, she said, "I am Toby Lee. I am a mean, rotten little kid. I have stolen my baby sister's bink. And now I am running from my dad! It is dark, and I am excited, and he is going to catch me any second! *Whee!*"

We watched the candle bounce one-two-three down the stairs, but before it even reached the bottom, it stopped. There was a *plink*—the sound of a jar lid landing. And then Yasmeen sighed and said, "We have got to be the dumbest smart kids yet. It's totally obvious. The bink is in the recycling bin."

Chapter Twenty

Yasmeen was right.

We hauled the recycling bin up to the kitchen and dumped the contents by the window so we could see. There were newspapers, bottles, foil, and cans. There was the jar lid. There was cat hair. And there, at the bottom, was Baby Alex's pink bink.

Yasmeen washed it and presented it to Mr. Lee. Then, with all of us interrupting each other, we explained how we had found it, and while we did that, Uncle Scott came into the kitchen.

"Is there any of that orange cake stuff left over?" he asked. Then he noticed the recycling bin. "Uh . . . whaddaya got that out for? Here—it's heavy. I can put it away for you. Basement stairs, right?"

I told him we had found the bink and said he didn't need to bother with the bin, we could do it, but he was already trying to take it.

"Thanks," I said. "But wait a sec—let me get the newspaper back in." Some pages were still on the floor, and when I bent down, I noticed one that wasn't from a newspaper at all. It was normal paper with typing on it. Something about it made my heart thump. It looked an awful lot like . . . I reached down to grab it, but Yasmeen was faster.

"*Bud!* This is it—the recipe—Grandma's pumpkin pie!"

Yasmen and Sofie whooped, I hollered, and all three of us high-fived. Then we called for Dad and Zooey Bonjour. They both came running, along with Mom and Grandma, and pretty soon it seemed all the guests were in the kitchen crowding around and squealing. When things had calmed down a little, Dad took the recipe himself and read it out loud: "Eggs, pumpkin, sugar, salt, cinnamon, nutmeg, ginger, cloves, cream. . . ." When he finally came to the clue for the secret ingredient, he shook his head. "Of *course!*" he said. "I can't believe I forgot!"

"What's it say? What's it say?" I tried to look over his shoulder.

"Comes from a legume." He paused dramatically. "*Not* from a bovine. Two words."

Yasmeen frowned, thinking.

I had no intention of thinking. "What's the answer?"

Dad opened his mouth, but Zooey shushed him: "Don't give it away, Dan. Remember—part of the fun will be your revealing it for the first time to my viewers on Saturday."

Dad nodded and zipped his finger across his lips.

I was disappointed, but still . . . I could wait till Saturday. Meanwhile, everyone was congratulating us, even Bub, whose services as understudy for *The Zooey Bonjour Show* were now officially at an end.

Bub picked up a wooden spoon from the kitchen counter and pretended he was a TV news reporter with a microphone. "So tell us, famous Chickadee Court Detectives, how did you crack the case this time?" He put the spoon up to Yasmeen's mouth.

"Uh . . ." Yasmeen looked at me, and Bub shifted the spoon to my mouth.

"Mr. Parakeet? Perhaps you'd like to comment for our viewers?"

Before I could think of a thing to say, Sofie grabbed the spoon and put it up to her own mouth. "I'll comment!" she said in her usual earsplitting voice. "The Chickadee Court Detectives have no idea how they found the recipe, and they have no idea who stole it, either! Getting it back just now—that was total dumb luck!"

Pretty soon after that, the power came back on. And then, one by one, the guests left. By five thirty, everyone was gone except Yasmeen. She had decided that even though the recipe was found, she still wanted to do the handwriting comparison. It was driving her crazy that we hadn't really solved the case, and even more crazy that Sofie was right.

With the mystery letter, the place cards, and the recipes from my mom's party, the two of us sat down at my mom's desk in the family room. Some of the cards we could set aside without even looking at them. Those were the ones that belonged to people who couldn't have written a letter thanking Zooey for inviting them to be on the show: all the kids, my parents, Zooey herself, my grandma, and—after what we had found out at the Knightly Tiger Inn—Mr. Stone. I thought we could throw out Ari's parents, too. They weren't at my mom's party, and we were pretty sure that was when the recipe disappeared.

That left us with eight possibilities: Officer Krichels, Bub, Mr. Lee, Mr. and Mrs. Sikora, Uncle Scott, Aunt Kate, and Mrs. Aaron.

Before that afternoon, I had never really looked that much at handwriting. Now I discovered there are all different varieties—up and down, slanty, fat, run-together, bumpy, scrunched-up, tidy. . . .

The writing in the mystery letter was stretched out and bold; Yasmeen called it "expansive." Both Officer Krichels's and Uncle Scott's were kind of the same style, but Officer Krichels's was too tall, and Uncle Scott's was too sloppy.

The best match turned out to be Mrs. Aaron's, but it wasn't perfect, either. Like when the mystery writer wrote "EAT network," the capital A was like a regular typed capital, but the *A* in Mrs. Aaron's signature was like an oversized lowercase *a*.

"That might just be her signature," Yasmeen said. "Sometimes people write their signatures different from their regular writing. Let's compare it to her recipe."

We looked through the recipes we had organized for Zooey and found Mrs. Aaron's for apricot-okra chutney filed under "Other." Too bad we had forgotten one thing. Unlike the rest, it wasn't handwritten. Mrs. Aaron has recipes for some of the foods she sells at the farm shop printed out on cards, and what she had left was one of those cards.

By this time, my eyes were getting dizzy, plus I was starting to think about dinner—as in would there be any, or were a couple of plates of Thanksgiving food really supposed to hold me till tomorrow morning? Didn't my parents realize I am a growing boy?

Yasmeen said we should take one more look in case we had missed something, so we got out Officer Krichels's place card and were discussing the way he makes his lowercase *e*'s when the doorbell rang.

My mom was zonked out in the living room. My dad was upstairs, so I got the door. Standing on the front step was Mrs. Aaron, and she looked annoyed. "I do apologize for bothering your family again, Alex," she said, and I noticed her hair was even more messed up than usual, plus she had a black smudge on her cheek. "But that blasted truck of mine is dead as a doornail."

"Jewel, have you been out there in the cold this whole time?" Dad had heard the bell and was coming down the stairs.

Mrs. Aaron stomped the snow off her boots. "I thought I could get it started if I went under the hood," she said, "but no dice." She came inside and explained she had already called the auto club from her cell, but they had so many calls with the bad weather that they couldn't be sure when they'd get to her.

"Bub's got jumper cables," Dad said, "and so does Professor Jensen. Somebody'll get you fixed up. You go warm up by the fire, and I'll check around."

Mrs. Aaron tugged off her boots, then went into the living room to talk to Mom. Dad got on the phone. Yasmeen pulled me aside. "This is our chance, bud! Since she's here, we can get another handwriting sample."

"I don't think it's a match," I said.

"It's closer than anybody else's," Yasmeen replied. "I know! We'll ask her to write out the recipe."

"The million-dollar pumpkin pie recipe?"

"Your dad *needs* a copy. He can't risk losing it again."

On a one-to-ten scale of dumb Yasmeen ideas, this one ranked an eleven. But already Yasmeen had taken a piece of lined notebook paper from the pile on my mom's desk, and now she was on her way to the kitchen to grab the green recipe binder.

"Fine," I said, following her. "If you want to totally embarrass yourself asking Mrs. Aaron for a favor that makes no sense, it's okay with me."

Mrs. Aaron and my mom had been talking, but when Yasmeen and I walked into the living room, they both stopped and looked up.

"Mrs. Aaron?" Yasmeen said in her sweetest voice. "Alex has a favor he wants to ask you."

"*Me?!*" I said.

"He's a little embarrassed about it," Yasmeen said. "Go ahead, Alex. She won't be mad."

"Mad about what?" Mrs. Aaron said.

To get it over with, I talked fast. "Would you mind copying out the pumpkin pie recipe for my dad?"

There was a pause. Then my mom gave me the exact "What the heck?" look such a dumb request deserved, but Mrs. Aaron said, "I don't mind. I don't like to be idle." Then she opened up the binder, positioned the blank paper, and started to write. After a few lines, she looked up. "It is a little ironic that you'd ask me of all people, though."

Yasmeen looked at me. " 'Ironic' means—"

"I *know* what it means," I said, which I actually did because we had studied irony in English class, and it means something's funny because it's the opposite of what you expect. "How come?" I asked Mrs. Aaron.

"Only that I'm the *last* person to be fooling around with recipes—I am such a terrible cook." She shook her head. "I live on canned soup, and half the time I burn that."

Yasmeen frowned. "Really? But I thought it was an Aaron family recipe.'"

"That part is true," Mrs. Aaron said. "But a woman over in Saucersburg does the actual cooking for me. Heck, I know how super-gourmet that chutney's supposed to be, but I won't even eat the stuff."

I couldn't help it. I grinned: *So there, Yasmeen!* Just like I told you—it was never Mrs. Aaron at all! I mean, everybody knows Zooey Bonjour only invites cooks on her show, never people who burn canned soup.

Chapter Twenty-one

I was feeling pretty pleased with myself at that moment, but then I saw how droopy Yasmeen looked—all collapsed in one of the living room chairs. I guess I couldn't blame her. The way the investigation was going, every one of her theories had been wrong.

Mrs. Aaron went back to writing. She laughed when she got to the clue part.

"A bovine's a cow," she said, "and a legume's a bean. Any farmer knows that. But what the ingredient is, I have no idea. I never could understand who's got the time to do crossword puzzles. On a farm, there's always work."

Mom said that sounded like her job. A minute later, I heard the sound of the front door opening and someone stomping in the hall. Then Bub—looking a lot like the abominable snowman—appeared in the living room doorway.

"I wouldn't've thought it was possible," he told Mrs. Aaron. "But your old truck is even sorrier than mine— won't start for nothin'. How about you let me give you a ride home now, and then you can get a tow tomorrow, when the weather's settled down some?"

Mrs. Aaron said she didn't want to inconvenience anybody, and Bub said he didn't mind, and Mrs. Aaron said the farm's such a long drive, and Bub said he wasn't busy, and she said what about the snow, and he said he'd learned to drive in snow—and they were totally back and forth like that till eventually she said yes, which everybody knew she was going to do in the first place. It's amazing to think how much time would be saved if grown-ups stopped being so polite.

Meanwhile, Dad had gone outside, probably to shovel the driveway. He didn't come back till after Bub and Mrs. Aaron had left, and when he did, he was grinning. "The all-new, spiffed-up Bub. He's quite the ladies' man!"

"So it's Mrs. Aaron now?" my mom asked.

"But what about Grandma?" I asked.

"I guess Bub's playing the field," Dad said. "Nothing wrong with that. . . . *Hey*!" He ducked the sofa pillow Mom threw. Yasmeen and I cracked up.

When Dad saw the neat copy of the recipe that Mrs. Aaron had made, he was pleased—even if she had used a fresh sheet of paper and not recycled scratch paper, as he would have. "I think I'll put that one in the binder. The other one's so beat up, you can hardly read it," he said.

By now, it was almost time for Yasmeen to go home. We settled ourselves back at Mom's desk in the family room and took another look at Officer Krichels's *e*'s and the way Bub tilts his capital *I*'s. Seeing them after a break, I didn't think either one was a match for the mystery writer, and Yasmeen admitted she didn't, either. Yasmeen put the place cards back in their original envelope to take home.

She was getting ready to go when Dad called from the living room, "Hey, don't I owe the Chickadee Court Detective Agency some pie as payment for finding that recipe?"

"We don't deserve it." Yasmeen tugged her hat down over her ears. "Sofie was right—it was luck."

"Luck or not"—now Dad was standing in the doorway—"you guys worked hard. How about million-dollar pie for lunch tomorrow? I'll be practice-baking all day anyway."

"Aren't you getting sick of making pies, Dad?" I asked.

"Not me," he said. "But there is a chance I'll wear out the rolling pin."

Chapter Twenty-two

There are good things and bad things about owning a cat.

If you want to know a good thing, it would be how that night Luau kept his big warm furry self right next to my head while I slept, and at four A.M., when the *beep-beep-beep* of the snow plow woke me, it was cozy to feel him there.

But if you want to know a bad thing, it would be how when it got light and I could have slept in, Luau woke me with a tail to the face that meant: *Look, Alex! It's a beautiful sunny day out!*

Who could sleep after that?

Downstairs, the house was quiet and sad compared to all the excitement of the day before. Just about the only reminder that Thanksgiving had ever happened was Great-grandma's silverware, laid out on dish towels on the kitchen table, ready to be put back in the chest. Also on the table was a note from Dad.

Mom's at work. (Surprise!) I've gone to the store for the secret ingredient. (No fair peeking when I get home!) Mrs. Aaron is going to make a pumpkin delivery some-

time this morning and get her truck, so don't be sur-prised. Love you—Dad

The note made me smile. There weren't any abbre-viations, and he had used lots of parentheses and excla-mation points. Being an experienced detective, I knew that meant he was in a good mood.

I poured myself a bowl of Pirate Crunchies, then—after I had made Luau promise not to breathe in my face for twenty-four hours—I gave him a Cheesy Dean. He didn't even thank me, just took it and ran. I think he was afraid I might change my mind.

By the time Mrs. Aaron rang the doorbell, I had gone upstairs, gotten dressed, and come down again. When I opened the door, I saw Luau had been right—it was a beautiful sunny day, bright blue sky and glittering snow. Bub was standing behind Mrs. Aaron, a load of pumpkins in his arms.

"I told him he didn't have to carry 'em," Mrs. Aaron said, "that I'm perfectly capable, but—"

"She just hates to have anybody do for her!" Bub said. "It was all she could do not to wrench the steering wheel out of my—"

"Well, if you'd only taken the back road the way I—"

"We'd be upside down in a ditch somewhere, so it's lucky—"

"Good morning, Bub. Good morning, Mrs. Aaron," I said.

But they had already walked past me toward the kitchen where Bub dumped the pumpkins on the counter. I followed them and did a quick count: seven. That would make a lot of Thanksgiving pies.

"I've got more where these came from," Mrs. Aaron said. "I had a bumper crop this year."

"Oh, I know," I said, thinking about how hard Yasmeen and I had worked on Monday at the farm.

"Is your dad around someplace?" Mrs. Aaron asked. "I've been thinkin' I might make him a little business proposition."

"Gone to the store," I explained.

"Have him give me a call, would you, Alex? Truck's already been towed, and my own personal chauffeur here's gonna take me home."

Bub grinned. "You'd do the same for me, wouldn't you, Jewel?"

Mrs. Aaron said, "Nope," but then she winked.

Yuck! I thought. Bub and Mrs. Aaron were arguing the way my parents do sometimes—and that meant romance, for sure. I hoped Grandma wouldn't be too disappointed.

* * *

When Dad came home, I offered to help bring in the groceries, but he figured out I was snooping for the secret ingredient and chased me away. I had to call through the kitchen door about phoning Mrs. Aaron.

"Will do!" he called back. "Now, go away!"

I settled in for some serious Lousy Luigi, and a few minutes later Luau found me and curled up in my lap. My Luigi guy had successfully sailed across a tomato sauce sea when Dad came into the family room. His apron was spotted orange with pumpkin, and there were white flour handprints on his jeans.

"Mrs. Aaron wants to sell my pies at the farm store!" he said. "What do you think of that?"

"Will we finally get rich?" I asked.

"Rich is not the point," Dad said.

"Then what is?" I said.

"Your mom and your grandma say it's time I went back to work. What do you say?"

I thought for a minute. "It's nice having you around, especially 'cause Mom never is. But if you were making pies, you'd still be home, right? So go for it!"

By now, the Thanksgiving pies in the oven were beginning to smell good. I took an extra big sniff, but I still couldn't detect anything secret—just the usual pumpkin. When the doorbell rang, I moved my sleeping lump of a cat—*Mrrf*—and went to answer it.

I had barely turned the knob before Yasmeen plunged inside. She was pumped. "We've been going about this investigation all wrong, bud," she announced. "It's time to stop rushing; slow down and do it right."

"Good afternoon, Yasmeen."

"Are you listening to me?"

"Do it right—check. But first, how 'bout some lunch?"

In the kitchen, Dad told us the pies would have to cool before he could cut pieces. Then he yawned. "I got up at six, and I've been going full-tilt ever since," he said. "I'm heading upstairs to shave and maybe do some laundry wrangling. Would you guys mind putting Grandma's silverware away? I'm gonna have to ramp up production later, and I'll need that space on the table."

Mom had explained to me about silver yesterday. It's not only polishing—you have to take extra-good care of it all the time, store it in a soft box so it won't get scratched, make sure it's totally dry, not a drop of water, when you put it away. That's why now the pieces were laid out on towels. It didn't take me and Yasmeen long to put it away, though. Each utensil had its own spot in the chest, the way hammers and screwdrivers do in a toolbox.

I was about to zip the chest closed for another year

when Yasmeen said, "Wait a sec, bud. Isn't this where you found those old recipes of your great-grandma's yesterday? Are they still in here somewhere?"

The recipes! I couldn't believe I had forgotten about them. "Dad said he was going to use the one for gravy. . . ." I looked around. "There it is—on the recipe stand."

"Let's compare the pie recipe in the newspaper to the one in the binder," Yasmeen said. "Who knows, maybe we can figure out the secret ingredient."

With the old newspaper page and the recipe binder, we sat down at the table. This is the recipe from the newspaper:

Pumpkin Pie
Unbaked 9-inch pie shell
3 eggs
2 cups mashed, cooked pumpkin
$\frac{1}{4}$ cup brown sugar
$\frac{1}{2}$ cup granulated sugar
$\frac{1}{4}$ teaspoon salt
$\frac{1}{2}$ teaspoon cinnamon
$\frac{1}{2}$ teaspoon nutmeg
$\frac{3}{4}$ teaspoon ground ginger
Dash ground cloves
1 $\frac{1}{4}$ cups light cream

Preheat oven to 350°F. In a large bowl, beat eggs. Add pumpkin, sugar, and spices. Beat well. Gradually blend in cream. Pour into prepared shell, and bake 65 minutes or until it tests done.

Grandma's pumpkin pie recipe was exactly the same except it had ¼ cup of "comes from a legume, not from a bovine (two words)" and ¼ cup less of cream. "So the secret ingredient replaces a liquid," Yasmeen said. "Maybe soy milk? That's two words, and soybeans are legumes. At least I think they are. Did your dad try that?"

"He was going to try tofu," I said, "but it's only one word." I shook my head. "This is *almost* as bad as detecting."

Yasmeen got a funny look on her face. "That reminds me," she said slowly. She flipped the newspaper page over, and there, on the other side, was a half-completed crossword puzzle. She looked up, and I knew we were having the identical same thought. "Wouldn't it be funny—?"

We were excited now, and one by one we read through the clues until we got to 21 Down: *Comes from a legume, not from a bovine. (Two words.)*

I closed my eyes just long enough to pray: *Help us out,*

Great-grandma! Then I moved my finger to the crossword grid and saw that 21 Down had twelve letters. Great-grandma had only filled in five of them:

_ E A N _ _ B _ _ _ _ R.

But combined with the clue, those five letters were enough.

Yasmeen shook her head. "Jeremiah," she said, "is never gonna believe it."

Chapter Twenty-three

We were pretty excited about figuring out the secret ingredient. Yasmeen said she was going to tell Sofie at the last possible minute, right before *The Zooey Bonjour Show* started. Then we agreed we wouldn't say anything to my dad. He might feel bad if he knew the secret had been revealed before the show.

Now, against my better judgment, I agreed we could take one last stab at identifying the recipe thief. It was Yasmeen's idea to reenact the crime.

Together we sat down at the table—smelling the mouth-watering smell of the cooling pies—and wrote a list of the props we needed: the binder, the spaghetti sauce pot, the birthday cake pan, two wineglasses, a bowl of Cheesy Deans, a broom, a dish towel, and Luau.

It didn't take long to set everything up the way it had been on Saturday. The spaghetti pot, the cake pan, and the bowl for the Cheesy Deans were on the kitchen table. The binder and the wineglasses were on the kitchen counter. The broom we left in the closet, and the dish towel was hanging on the handle of the oven door.

Luau had been asleep on the sofa in the family room. Now I brought him into the kitchen, set him down in the corner, and explained what he was supposed to do.

He washed his face.

Then I opened the bag of Cheesy Deans, and all of a sudden, he got very interested. *What was it you wanted, Alex? Back flips? Cartwheels? Tail stands? You got it!*

I said all he had to do was leap into the spaghetti pot the way he did on the night of Mom's birthday, then run across the cake pan and jump across to the kitchen counter—knocking down the wineglasses and the recipe binder—then jump down to the floor. After that, he could run down the basement stairs if he wanted, but that part was optional.

"If you do all that just right, I will give you a Cheesy Dean," I said.

Luau looked at me, then I blinked a long slow blink. *One single Cheesy Dean for a veritable circus act? Are you joking?*

It took some negotiating, but finally we settled on two Cheesy Deans now plus two bonus Cheesy Deans every day till the bag was gone.

After that, Luau swished his tail, which meant, *Just so I get this straight—would you mind demonstrating for me, Alex?*

"What's he saying?" Yasmeen asked.

"You'll see," I said, and did my best approximation

of a cat leap toward the table, stuck my hand in the spaghetti pot, trailed it across the cake pan, waved it through the air, and dragged it along the counter.

Yasmeen laughed so hard, she had to hold her stomach.

When I got to the wineglasses, I realized it would be better if we substituted plastic cups, so I got some out and set that part up again. Then I looked at Luau. "Got it?"

He got in pounce position and swished his tail: *I can do this in one take.*

"Lights! Camera! And . . . *action!*" Yasmeen said.

It wasn't a perfect reenactment. It turns out that it's harder for a cat to climb out of a spaghetti pot when there's no spaghetti in it. And then when Luau hit cake pan, it skidded like a skateboard and he almost wiped out.

Still, in spite of the glitches, we did learn several important things. Like, we saw that Luau must have hit the recipe binder as he ran forward across the counter, so that it fell ahead of him and landed on the floor. Then when he jumped down, he ran across the pages, leaving the spaghetti sauce paw prints.

Meanwhile, the plastic cups, playing the part of wineglasses, crashed behind him.

When Luau's part was done, Yasmeen walked to the corner by the back door and held an imaginary DS game in her hand. "Now I'm Michael Jensen," she said, and then she said her line: "Did something just happen?"

Playing the part of everybody else in the room, I cracked up.

"And now"—Yasmeen grabbed the broom from the closet and swept up the plastic cups—"I'm your grandma."

"Okay," I said. "And I'll be me." I took the dish towel from the handle on the oven door and wiped pretend spaghetti sauce off the table.

That was where we were when Dad, yawning and rubbing his eyes, walked into the kitchen. This was actually kind of weird because on the night of the party, he and Mom had walked into the kitchen at right about this point in the action. Probably that's what made me remember something else: Uncle Scott picking the recipe binder up from the floor.

"Now I'm being Uncle Scott," I said to Yasmeen, which probably sounded pretty weird to Dad. I picked up the binder, and when I did, I noticed the spaghetti sauce paw print on the front of the pitty-pink pudding recipe. Of course, there were no marks at all on the back of the pumpkin pie recipe because it was the new copy, the one Mrs. Aaron made yesterday.

Having napped, Dad was behind schedule. Would we mind waiting till he got some pies in the oven for payment? We said okay and went into the family room. Luau was already there, stretched out on the back of the sofa. He flicked his tail, which meant, *I believe the Oscar nominations are due in January?*

I told him that unfortunately there's no category for stunt kitties.

Meanwhile, Yasmeen dropped into the recliner. Of course, her brain was in its usual hyperdrive. "All along, we figured Uncle Scott couldn't have stolen the recipe because he doesn't care about food or recipes. But he *is* the one who picked up the binder," she said. "We *should* have considered him. We should have considered everyone! The whole problem with our investigation has been that we didn't cast a wide enough net."

"What do you mean?"

"Think about it, bud. First we focused on Zooey and Mr. Stone, and then we focused on Mrs. Aaron. What we should have done was investigate *everybody* who had the means and the opportunity to take the recipe."

"That would be everybody who was at our house for the birthday party," I said. "But we couldn't. We didn't have time."

"And now we do!" Yasmeen said. "Of course, now we know it couldn't be your uncle and aunt. Their handwriting didn't match the mystery letter. But we still have plenty of suspects. I say we start with the Jensens and the Ryans. Didn't they look at the recipe binder that night? And Michael Jensen really liked Cheesy Deans, remember?"

Yasmeen is my best friend who happens to be a girl, but no way was I going to spend my Thanksgiving vacation going door-to-door accusing our neighbors and asking for handwriting samples. I told Yasmeen that, and she said, "But it's a matter of justice!"

"No, it's not," I said. "You just can't stand that Sofie's right."

Yasmeen said that was unfair. I said unfair didn't mean untrue. Things were heating up good when Dad called us into the kitchen. I thought we'd declare a truce over pie and milk, but the table was bare. While Yasmeen and I had been talking, I had heard the phone ring twice, and now Dad said, "I'm sorry kids. I'll have to give you a rain check on the pie. Mrs. Aaron called. She already has orders, and I can't spare even a single one."

I asked him who the other call was from, and he grinned. "Uncle Scott and Aunt Kate. They have extra tickets to the game tomorrow, and they invited your mom and me. I'm psyched—it's the biggest game of the year!"

Chapter Twenty-four

The sound of the garage door woke me the next morning, and even though it was my dad's big day, I felt grumpy. I hate fighting with Yasmeen, and when she had left yesterday we were both still mad. I rolled over to go back to sleep, but a few seconds later, I heard Dad's feet on the stairs, and then he came into my room. "Rise and shine, sleepyhead," he said. "I've already been out and about."

I propped myself up on my elbows. "To the farm?"

Dad nodded. "We bakers rise at dawn. Hey, that's a good one! Bakers rise? Like bread?"

It was much too early in the morning for Dad jokes. "What time do we have to be at the stadium?" I asked.

The game was at 4:00 he explained, and Zooey's show would be broadcasting live from 2:30 to 3:00. She and Grandma wanted him at the TV stage they had set up outside the north end of the stadium at 1:00 sharp.

Mom had already gone to work—surprise. The plan was she'd work a half day, then meet us to watch the show live at the stadium. When I came downstairs a while later,

I saw she had forgotten her lunch—left it next to the recipe binder on the kitchen counter. I pointed this out to Dad, and he laughed. "That's not her lunch."

"What is it, then?" I asked.

"Never mind!" Dad said. "And don't peek."

The way he said it, I figured right away the paper lunch sack held the "secret ingredient," and he had put it out so he wouldn't forget to take it to the stadium. Little did Dad know I wasn't tempted to peek one bit.

In case you don't know about tailgates, I will tell you. The idea is that before a football game, people come and eat a picnic in the parking lot outside the stadium. It used to be that people had trucks or station wagons, and folded down the tailgates for a table. That's where the name comes from. But now people mostly bring real tables—along with coolers and chairs and awnings and surround-sound systems and televisions and propane grills and . . .

A little after noon, a car picked Dad up to take him to the stadium. A few minutes later, I had a terrible thought—my dad can be so absentminded!—and I checked the kitchen counter. The binder and the paper bag were gone.

Mom was going to get a ride over from work as soon as she could. Meanwhile, I was meeting a bunch of people at Bub's corner at 1:30 so we could walk over together. Some of our neighbors—like Yasmeen's parents—weren't going to go to the stadium to watch the show live at all. Instead, they were watching it on TV in their warm houses. I couldn't blame them.

Bub, Sofie Sikora, Mr. Stone, and Jeremiah were already waiting when I got to the corner. I asked Bub where Mrs. Aaron was, and he said she was going to work at the farm store up to the last minute, then drive herself over to the stadium.

By now, Yasmeen had joined us. "But where will she park? You can't get within a mile of the stadium on a football day."

"Her truck's still out of commission, so she's takin' that old motorcycle of hers," Bub said. "She can park it right by the stage if she wants to. I told her it was dangerous to drive it on a slippery day like this, but of course she wouldn't listen." He looked around. "Are we all here? Where's Marjie Lee? I hear she finally got back okay."

"Coming!" She was jogging toward us and waving. She had a diaper bag over her shoulder and Baby Alex bouncing in the backpack.

"No Toby?" Bub asked.

"Home with his dad," she answered.

"Thank goodness," Mr. Stone whispered.

We started walking, and I fell in next to Sofie. "I thought you were grounded."

She said, "Not anymore. I promised my parents I'd never do anything bad again."

"And they believed you?" I asked.

"Of course not," Sofie said. "But they were sick of having me home all the time."

The snow that had been so pretty and white was dirty gray now. We had to sidestep ice puddles on the sidewalk. Behind me, Yasmeen was talking to Mrs. Lee. "How was your trip?" Yasmeen asked.

"Relaxing, and I learned a lot. You and Alex were kind to help out. I know Mr. Lee really appreciated Thanksgiving."

Yasmeen said, "It was no trouble."

Jeremiah said, *"What?"* but Yasmeen shushed him. Then she turned to me. "I've been thinking, bud. You're right."

I looked up at her. "Say that again. The cold must be affecting my ears."

She punched my arm. "I still want to know who stole that recipe. But it's not worth getting all the neighbors upset again. And it's not worth fighting with you, either."

So why hadn't she agreed with me yesterday? I really, *really* wanted to ask her that, but Yasmeen had done something hard by admitting she was wrong. So all I said was, "That's what I think, too."

And after that, I felt a lot more cheerful.

You can't see the stadium from my house because it's over a hill. But the walk is only about a mile, twenty minutes if you keep moving. As we got closer, there were barriers to keep out cars, and we joined with the mob walking down the middle of the street. In the distance was the sound of the Knightly Tiger Band. I saw college students with tiger-striped faces, college students wearing tiger ears, college students wearing tiger tails.

Zooey's show was being broadcast from a temporary stage set up north of the stadium. Walking through the tailgate crowd, we kept seeing people we knew who offered us chips and wings and cookies. Finally, Bub looked at his watch and announced that we'd miss the whole show if we didn't hurry.

We tried to move faster, but just below the press boxes, a kid's voice called, "Hey, Jer'miah!" and Jeremiah called, "Hey, Micah!" And a second later, the two of them were tackling each other.

Micah's family had an RV with a tiger-striped awning on the side and a picnic table under the awning. There were loads of people there, and in the center was Mrs. Levin, holding Baby Jack. "Come on over and have some lunch!" she called to Yasmeen and me. "I've got a fresh jar of peanut butter!"

Yasmeen corralled Jeremiah. I said, "We can't stop!"

Mrs. Levin smiled and waved. "I understand! We're gonna watch Zooey Bonjour on TV right here. And have you heard? She's got a surprise guest for her viewers today."

A surprise guest? But that was Dad . . . right?

A few minutes later we rounded the north end of the stadium and saw our destination—a huge white canopy and underneath it, rising out of the dirty snow, a pink and turquoise kitchen on a stage about six feet off the ground. Above the stage, can-shaped TV lights dangled from metal scaffolding. In front of it, there were chairs for the audience and three big cameras. Behind the stage was a banner that said: CHEESY DEANS, THE CHEESY CRACKER WITH FISHY GOODNESS, PRESENTS *The Zooey Bonjour Show*!

Beyond the stage was a TV truck like the ones the sports guys use and also a smaller pink RV with Zooey's picture on the side. In the picture, she was holding a bowl of Cheesy Deans and smiling. The picture was so big that the crackers looked like sharks.

Zooey and Grandma were already on the stage. Zooey looked perfect, as usual—only today she was perfect and wearing a pink apron. Grandma was fiddling with a microphone clipped to Zooey's collar.

And where was Dad? Did he have to put makeup on, the way Zooey did? I had this sudden terrible vision of him in the pink RV having his eyebrows plucked.

Mom waved from the front row of the audience. Officer Krichels had dropped her off, and she had saved seats for us. We joined her and sat down. A couple of rows behind us were Aunt Kate and Uncle Scott, plus a lot of other people I knew. Everybody wanted to wave and say hi like I was some kind of celebrity, too.

We watched the stagehands set out the paper bag and the recipe binder next to a bowl, a spoon, a whisk, a rolling pin, a box of wax paper, and a pink canister of flour. I could hear other people in the audience trying to guess what was in the bag.

"That's the secret ingredient, isn't it?" Sofie whispered. "Did you peek?"

Yasmeen grinned a smug little grin. "We didn't have to. Alex and I used our superior detective skills to figure it out on our own."

"Then *tell* me!" Sofie leaned over, and Yasmeen whispered in her ear. Sofie giggled. "You're kidding, right? But that's so *boring*!"

Just as a voice on a speaker was saying, "Places, everybody," I heard the roar of an engine and looked up. Bouncing across the field was Mrs. Aaron on her motorcycle, heading right for us. A few seconds later, she cut the engine and rolled to a stop, then pulled off her helmet, propped up the bike, and ran toward us to take the seat Bub had saved.

"Ready, Zooey?" said the voice on the speaker. "Everyone? Ten seconds."

The lights on the cameras lit the stage. Zooey nodded, patted her hair, tugged her apron, looked up, smiled, and called, "Bonjour, Knightly Tiger fans!"

And we all answered, "Bonjour, Zooey Bonjour!"

"I can't say how pleased I am to be tailgating outside Tiger Stadium, where the Knightly Tigers are playing Ohio later this afternoon! Now, we have a lot to pack into our thirty-minute show, so without further ado, I am going to introduce our special guest star!"

I was totally expecting Zooey to say, "Dan Parakeet!" or, better yet, "Alex Parakeet's dad, Dan!" But what she actually said was, *"Knightly Tiger Head Coach, Jack Patronelli!"*

And with that, the world-famous football coach himself came out from behind a curtain and trotted onto the stage to receive Zooey's one-cheek, two-cheek kiss while the audience went crazy.

Coach Patronelli? *Oh* . . . he must be who Mrs. Levin was talking about, her own dad! But what was he doing there? And where was *my* dad?

The coach waved to us fans, and Zooey said,

"Thanks so much for taking time out right before a big game."

"Wouldn't have missed it," Coach Patronelli said. "In the past few years, I've become a big fan of your show. Your chicken paprika is one of my specialties."

Under her breath, Yasmeen said, "Chicken paprika?"

"I understand you're also a fan of a certain extraordinary Thanksgiving pie!" Zooey said. "The creation of today's guest chef!"

And suddenly, it came to me. Coach Patronelli was the writer of the mystery letter! And he wasn't *replacing* my dad on the show—he had *suggested* my dad for the show!

Now Zooey introduced, "Da-a-a-n Parakeet!" and Dad trotted up to the stage himself. I guess it must have made me nervous to see him up there, because a minute later, Yasmeen leaned over and whispered, "You're turning blue, Alex. *Breathe!*"

Zooey asked Dad questions, and Dad told the story about the old recipe and selling the pie at the school auction. Then Jack Patronelli picked it up, explaining how his daughter had served the pie at Thanksgiving dinner.

Zooey said, "Can we get a close-up of the recipe?" and one of the cameras zoomed in on the binder so that the recipe appeared, neatly copied out in Mrs. Aaron's handwriting, bigger than life on all the TV monitors. What the monitors also showed was the facing page, the back side of the cherry-chocolate mousse recipe. Dad had printed out this particular recipe on scratch paper from when he and Aunt Kate had a business together. The page was an upside-down printout of an e-mail from Katharine Anne Parakeet, my aunt Kate, to Daniel Martin Parakeet, my dad. For the first time I noticed that the subject line said "Mayflower Project."

There was no time to read more, though. The camera pulled back, and on the stage Dad was saying, "The secret is the fresh pumpkin—not canned—and, of course, the ingredient written in code, an ingredient that I am going to reveal for the first time today!"

The audience clapped and cheered.

Next, Zooey Bonjour asked Dad his advice for making a flaky pie crust, and while he was explaining, he rolled out the dough in a perfect circle, lifted it cleanly off the counter, and laid it in the pie pan.

The audience oohed and aahed.

Zooey said, "We're going to take a little break, but we'll be right back to reveal for the very first time ever *the secret ingredient!*"

The lights on the cameras went dark, and the monitors showed a commercial for Cheesy Deans that featured wedges of cheddar cheese snorkeling among sardines. After that, the loudspeaker voice said, "Ten seconds," and Zooey patted her hair, tugged her apron, and looked at the camera.

The lights came up again. Zooey recapped the pie making so far, and then Dad talked about selecting and baking a fresh pumpkin, mentioning that he always acquired his fresh pumpkins from nearby Aaron Farm. Finally, all the other ingredients had been mixed, and it was time to reveal the secret. The audience held its breath. Dad unfolded the paper bag. Dad pulled the paper bag open. Then . . .

Dad froze. Beside him, Zooey looked into the bag, and her expression changed fast from puzzlement to scowl. "A cheese sandwich, carrot sticks, and an apple?" she said.

"Oops," Dad said.

Zooey inhaled, then she looked up at the camera and smiled her calmest, most plastic smile. "We'll be back after an additional word from our sponsor."

Sitting on the other side of Yasmeen, Jeremiah said, "Uh-oh," and Mom said, "I must have grabbed the wrong bag!" and Sofie said, "So where's the *right* bag?"

Mom closed her eyes and slumped back against her chair. "On my desk at work," she said. "I was so busy, I never had a chance to eat lunch!"

Chapter Twenty-five

The instant the lights on the cameras died, Zooey lost it—probably for the first time in her entire life. She yelled at Dad. She yelled at the stagehands. She even yelled at Coach Patronelli.

Somebody had to do something! They'd be back on the air in sixty seconds!

Like Dad, I was frozen—until Sofie Sikora jumped to her feet and tried to wrench my arm from its socket. *"Come on!"* With her other hand, she yanked Yasmeen, and before I knew it, the three of us were up out of our seats and running.

"Where are we going?" I yelled.

Sofie's answer was to speed up. Soon we had left *The Zooey Bonjour Show* behind and were entering the west parking lot, where a million tailgaters presented a total obstacle course for three kids in a hurry.

"Block for me, guys!" Sofie yelled.

"Where . . . ," I gasped, "did you say . . . we're going?"

Sofie looked back over her shoulder to answer and

almost tripped over a tiny person wearing a full Tiger cheerleader outfit. I grabbed one elbow, and Yasmeen got the other. Sofie spun around and kept going. The cheerleader never noticed.

Ten yards and a first down later, I saw the Levins' tiger-striped awning and beneath it Mrs. Levin herself. Sofie turned toward her, and that's when—*duh, Alex*—I got it.

"How did you get here so fast?" Mrs. Levin must have seen us coming. "What happened with your Dad, Alex? He looked like—"

"Peanut butter!" All three of us shouted at once.

I guess Mrs. Levin inherited her dad's quick-thinking, football-coaching genes because in four steps, she was in and out of the mobile home, a jar of peanut butter under her arm. She handed it off to me, and I lateraled it to Yasmeen.

We knew we were on a sixty-second clock with no timeouts. What would happen if the show returned from the commercial before we got back?

Once again, we rounded the north end of the stadium, and now we could see the stage. Were the camera lights back on? Not yet, but I saw Zooey was facing forward, straightening her apron and patting her hair.

"Dad!"

Yasmeen held up the peanut butter jar and at the

same instant hit a sloppy patch of snow. One foot slipped and she tumbled forward, tossing the peanut butter jar up and out of her hands.

Fumble!

If that jar fell and burst, we were done for. I reached for it, felt it at the tips of my fingers, and, with a super-human effort, managed to bring it in.

Fumble recovered by Alex Parakeet!

"Keep going!" Sofie shouted.

Yasmeen was on the ground, but I couldn't look back. The camera lights were on now, and Zooey was speaking.

"Dad!"

This time he heard me, looked up, and squinted in the glare of the lights. I was at the outer edge of the audience—close enough to recognize the stern expression on Zooey's otherwise perfect face as well as the frown of distress on my dad's. There were only a few minutes left in the show. Dad needed the secret ingredient, and he needed it *now*! I wished it was Yasmeen making the throw, but she was out of commission, so, with no choice, I took the heavy jar in my right hand, rocked back, cocked my arm, and launched a perfect Hail Mary pass, the most important one of my career to date.

Did I say perfect?

Not so much.

A big jar full of peanut butter is a whole lot heavier than a football full of air, and I guess its aerodynamic properties are different, too. Someday I will look this up. But just then, I watched the peanut butter jar arc over the audience and the cameras and drop down toward the stage, its motion nothing at all like a football's. It didn't help, either, that my receiver—Dad—was having a hard time seeing against the lights. Too late I realized that if my pass was incomplete, that big plastic jar would explode, splattering brown peanut goo all over Zooey Bonjour and her perfect pink-and-turquoise kitchen.

Zooey was not going to like that.

The audience could see better than Dad could, and as the jar hurtled forward, Bub's familiar voice shouted, "Incoming!"

Zooey's sensible response was to close her eyes and clasp her hands over her head. Dad put everything he had into stretching to make the catch . . . but it wasn't going to be enough. We were milliseconds away from a spatter disaster when a miracle occurred. Like a pro, Coach Jack Patronelli leaped . . . reached . . . got his fingertips on the jar, and . . . reeled it in!

"Touchdown!" Bub cried.

The crowd went wild.

*   *   *

"Now, *that's* what I call television!" Zooey Bonjour said a few minutes later. The show was over, the lights were turned off, the audience was beginning to disperse. "We are going to be all over the web in an hour. I see ratings and cookbook sales through the roof!"

In the midst of all the excitement, Mrs. Aaron's cell phone rang, and it was Judy at the farm store. "She wants to know how many pies you can deliver this week, Dan," Mrs. Aaron said. "She can't take orders fast enough!"

Dad said he'd start baking in a little more than three hours—right after the Knightly Tigers beat Ohio.

Meanwhile, everybody was swarming around to congratulate him on the show and me on my throw. Even Coach Patronelli came over. "You've got quite an arm, son. But straighten it out next time, okay?" Then he turned to say hi to Uncle Scott.

I tried to be excited and smiling and happy like everybody else, but what I really wanted to do was talk to Yasmeen. Oh, sure, an hour ago we had agreed it wasn't worth it to figure out who stole the recipe, but that was before that close-up of the e-mail appeared on the monitor. Something told me the close-up was just the clue we needed to solve the case at last.

Yasmeen's face was mud-spattered from her fall, and her jacket was dirty and wet. She was cold, but she wasn't hurt. "Are you thinking what I'm thinking?" she asked.

I nodded. "We need to take another look at the binder."

Dad had brought the recipe binder with him when he came offstage. When I pushed my way through his adoring fans, I saw the binder tucked under his arm.

"Can I have it?" Dad was so busy talking to everybody—reliving his big moment—that he handed it over without realizing it.

Bub had already herded the first part of Dad's neighborhood fan base back toward home. Sofie's parents were expecting her, so she was going with them. It was really Sofie who had saved the day for Dad, and I wanted to thank her, but that would have to wait.

Yasmeen and I had a case to solve.

We sat ourselves in the chairs where the audience had been, turned the binder upside down and for the first time read the back sides of the *Sweets* recipes. The pages were a series of e-mails between my dad and my aunt Kate, all dated November six years ago. That would have been when their business was falling apart.

Pretty quick, we realized all the messages were about new business ideas. In one with the subject line "Socks," Aunt Kate suggested starting a Sock-of-the-Month Club—a gift certificate for sending socks twelve times a year. "It would be a perfect present for grandparents to give their grandchildren!" Kate had written.

"Who wants socks?" I asked Yasmeen.

She shrugged. "You can't always tell what will work on the Internet."

"You mean like WereYouontheMayflower.com?"

The only recipe with nothing on the back was for pumpkin pie, of course, because this was Mrs. Aaron's new copy. Going backward through the alphabet, the next one, cherry-chocolate mousse, was the page that had been displayed in close-up on the TV monitor:

To: Daniel Martin Parakeet
From: Katharine Anne Parakeet
Re: Mayflower Project

Interesting idea, but I see a million problems—
not just with the marketing but the program-
ming. I say we keep trying.

Kate

"It's a reply," I said. "Aunt Kate's reply to an e-mail from Dad."

"So *his* e-mail must have been the one proposing the idea—the Mayflower Project."

My heart sank. "So WereyouontheMayflower.com was my dad's idea in the first place?"

Yasmeen nodded. "And your aunt and uncle stole it from him! Worse yet, they stole it twice—six years ago, and then again at your mom's party, when they realized the e-mail might give them away. . . . But wait a minute, wouldn't your dad remember that the original idea was his?"

I looked at her. "My dad?"

"Good point," Yasmeen said. "Anyway, one thing's for sure. We need to see the original of the recipe, the one that was stolen. We need to see for sure what's on the back."

It was getting close to game time. People were drifting away, but there were still fans hanging out with my new celebrity dad. I waved and called over to get his attention. "Did you save the original of Grandma's pumpkin pie recipe?"

I guess the question sounded weird out of the blue like that because Dad gave me a funny look. "Sure," he said after a pause. "Uh . . . top drawer of Mom's desk."

In a flash, I was on my feet, motioning to Yasmeen— Let's go! I was turning to start home when I heard a familiar high-pitched voice: my aunt Kate: "Scott?" she called. "*Oh, Scott!* Where did he go, anyway? He was here just a second ago!"

Chapter Twenty-six

With so many people everywhere, I hadn't even noticed Uncle Scott and Aunt Kate. But of course they were here. They were going to the game with my parents. And now it looked as if they had heard me ask about the recipe—and had heard my dad's answer, too.

If that was true, I was pretty sure I knew why Aunt Kate couldn't find her husband. He was hotfooting it to my house to get the recipe—the e-mail—and destroy it once and for all.

Did that mean Uncle Scott was the bad guy and not Aunt Kate? He had been the one to pick up the binder at my mom's party. And he was the one who had blue Cheesy Dean powder on his fingers—the powder that made the blue marks on the recipe. Or maybe Aunt Kate and he were in it together?

Sometimes Yasmeen and I don't have to talk. We just know. Now Yasmeen said, "There!" and pointed. In the distance, I could see a tall dark-haired man heading at a dead run toward the north parking lot.

"We'll never catch him!" I said. "He's got his Porsche, and all we've got are our feet."

The words were hardly out of my mouth when I heard a roar: Mrs. Aaron's motorcycle, revving up for departure. Yasmeen and I looked at each other. If we could do some very fast talking, plus get away before my mom saw us . . .

On the one hand, the ride to my house on the back of Mrs. Aaron's motorcycle was the most terrifying thing I have ever experienced.

On the other hand, it was the most fun.

Mrs. Aaron was carrying one spare helmet that she gave to me, and she handed hers over to Yasmeen. Now the three of us were squished on the seat, me clinging to Mrs. Aaron and Yasmeen clinging to me. Across the field we sped—my eyes shut tight. Then we bumped up onto the pavement, a plume of mud and slush spattering in our wake.

"Lean into the curves, kids! Don't fight the bike!" Mrs. Aaron called, and we veered left onto the roadway.

There was no traffic. By now, everyone in town was either in the stadium or in front of a TV set. Mrs. Aaron opened up the throttle, and the distance passed in a heart-stopping blur of wind, motion, and noise. Then, brief as a roller coaster ride, the trip came to an end, our arrival signaled by the squeal of rubber on the slippery asphalt in front of my house.

I took a breath—probably my first since climbing on the bike—and looked up. Uncle Scott's Porsche was in the driveway, steam rising off the hood.

Yasmeen saw it, too. "Hurry!"

We handed back the helmets than tried to run before we untangled ourselves from the bike. That didn't work so well. If Mrs. Aaron hadn't leaned hard—"*Whoa, there!*"— we all would have landed in the dirty snow by the curb.

"Thank you!" I called when we were finally free.

Halfway up the walk, I saw that the front door was ajar, and now I felt scared going into my own house. Before, it was always cool that my uncle, the former Knightly Tiger, was about seven feet tall and four feet wide, but at the moment, it didn't seem cool at all.

Without Yasmeen, I might have lost my nerve. As it was, we crossed the threshold together, and right away, from the front hall, I could hear drawers squeaking and slamming in the family room—the drawers of my mom's desk.

"Come on!" Yasmeen grabbed my elbow. I had taken exactly one step when Uncle Scott came barreling around the corner right at us. The sight of us startled him, but his football training came back. He faked left, dodged right, tried to get between Yasmeen and me . . .

but close quarters made this impossible, and, besides, Yasmeen and I had been working too long and too hard on this case to let the culprit get away now.

"Tackle!" Yasmeen went high and I went low. Uncle Scott's legs flew out from under him, and—*Oof!*—his big body hit the floor.

Yasmeen looked over at me, then down at Uncle Scott, who was lying on his side, eyes closed, head resting on one of my mom's snow boots.

"Are you okay?" she asked him.

"Flag on the play," he muttered. "Fifteen yards."

Yasmeen looked at me. "I think he's okay."

In Uncle Scott's right hand was a crumpled sheet of paper. I knelt down, pulled it from his fingers, and smoothed it out. Then Yasmeen and I read:

To: Katharine Anne Parakeet
From: Daniel Martin Parakeet
Subject: Mayflower Project

Hey, Sis—Idea of the morning—must be the time of year, but—what about we start a website to encourage people to study American history? It would be great for kids but other people, too. You log on and it tells you if you had an ancestor who came over on the

Mayflower! Visitors could enter their names and maybe their birthdays, then follow prompts . . . There could be historical information, too. In the end the screen answers: YES, you had an ancestor on the Mayflower, or: SORRY, probably not.

"Your dad was wrong." Uncle Scott was sitting up now. "It wasn't in the top drawer at all. It was in the third drawer on the right. That's why it took me so long to find it."

"Dad's memory strikes again," I said.

Uncle Scott rose to a standing position slowly, wiggled his body parts to test them out, then looked at his watch. "I gotta go."

Yasmeen crossed her arms over her chest. "Not till you confess."

Uncle Scott raised his hands in surrender. "Anything," he said, "so long as I don't miss the kickoff. What do I gotta sign?"

"Just admit you stole the recipe," I said.

"Of course I did!" Uncle Scott looked at his watch again. "Kate and I built that business. Who cares whose idea it was all those years ago? But I know how your family's always strapped for money, Alex. And I was afraid if your dad ever realized he had that e-mail—proof the whole thing was his idea—he'd want to claim half of what I had worked for. Now, that wouldn't be fair, would it?"

I didn't know about fair or about money. I only knew my uncle shouldn't have taken something from my dad. "Does Aunt Kate know you took it?" I asked.

Uncle Scott shook his head. "She doesn't know anything. Heck, all along I thought the idea was hers. Then I saw that paper in the recipe binder on the floor. I panicked. Can you blame me? I did the first thing I thought of, which was throw it in the recycling. Afterward, I figured that was that, so you can imagine I almost had heart failure when you kids dug it out at Thanksgiving. Then to top it off, today I see that other e-mail on TV during Zooey's show." He looked at his watch. "Now can I go?"

It didn't seem right that Uncle Scott could go and watch a football game when we had just caught him red-handed. But how were we supposed to stop him? No one was going to be driving up in a patrol car to handcuff him and haul him to jail. Stealing a recipe isn't much of a crime. And it's not like he had to break into my house just now, either. He and Aunt Kate have keys, just the way my parents have keys to their condo.

With no choice, Yasmeen and I let him go. We had solved the case, but now I had a new worry. How was I ever going to tell my mom and dad that my own uncle was the thief?

Chapter Twenty-seven

The way it turned out, I didn't have to tell them. Instead, Uncle Scott took the opportunity of the Knightly Tigers' exciting 16–14, come-from-behind victory over Ohio to do it for me.

"Aunt Kate cried," Mom told me that night.

Dad was in full pie production in the kitchen. Mom was sitting with me in the family room. "Kate is just like your dad," Mom explained. "She didn't remember anymore that Dad was the first to propose the Mayflower project. She thought she came up with the idea herself after she and Scott moved to Philadelphia."

"Is she telling the truth about that?" I asked.

"I think so," Mom said. "Ideas are tricky. Sometimes it's hard to remember what you heard from someone else and what you came up with on your own."

"So what happens now?" I asked.

"Kate said the only honorable thing would be for them to sign over the business to your dad and me."

"That means we're rich!" I said. And—I couldn't help it—right away I started a mental list of stuff to buy:

a huge flat-screen TV, new video games, the baseball bat my parents said was too expensive, football gloves, a Porsche like Uncle Scott's. . . .

But Mom interrupted my daydream. "Not so fast, hotshot. Your dad said no way. In fact—in spite of how mad we both are at Scott—we all agreed on one thing: Scott and Kate developed the business. They should reap most of the benefits."

"Most?" I said hopefully.

Mom smiled. "We'll be negotiating some kind of settlement. Kate is going to insist. I don't know how much yet, but Dad would like some capital to fix up the kitchen for his pie business. And he also wants me to take some time off. He thinks I work too much."

"You do!" I said. "If you hadn't been in such a hurry to get to work this morning, you never would've mixed up those paper bags."

"So I've been told," Mom said, "over and over, all day long."

The next week was crazy. Dad was making pies 24/7 and Mom had to work all the time, as usual, which meant I was eating a lot of Pirate Crunchies. Even shrimp stir-fry was starting to sound good.

Then there was the money thing. Every time Dad came back from another run to Aaron Farm, he brought with him a green plastic pouch full of cash and checks. Since we were also about to get the payment from WereYouontheMayflower.com, it felt like overnight our family had gone from worrying about money all the time to having more than we needed.

Outside my family, there was also news. Sofie Sikora started sitting with Yasmeen and me at lunch in the caf, and once she helped me with my math, too. I don't know exactly how, but I was kind of getting used to her. Was it possible someday we'd be friends?

Then there was Zooey Bonjour, famous TV chef. She didn't go back to Philadelphia right away after the show like she planned. Sofie, Yasmeen, and I couldn't figure out why till finally Grandma explained that Coach Jack Patronelli had asked her out to dinner after the game, and then asked her out on Sunday and Monday, too. Now they were an item.

This left Mr. Stone heartbroken . . . for about a day. With Bub seeing Mrs. Aaron, Grandma was available, so Mr. Stone invited her out for coffee.

Dad said, "You can't tell the players without a scorecard," which I think means sometimes even old people find romance. My question is: Why would they want to?

There was one more piece of news: Zooey Bonjour was looking for a new sponsor. The makers of Cheesy Deans had decided to "move in a different direction" with their marketing. I didn't understand what that meant till Grandma explained. Instead of selling Cheesy Deans as fishy crackers for people, they were going to start selling Cheesy Deans as fishy treats for cats. Luau wanted to audition for the job of spokes-kitty, but I convinced him he wouldn't like all that sunshine in Hollywood.

The following Saturday there was no football game. Dad had vowed to take a break from pie making, and Mom had promised not to go in to work—not even for an hour. Instead, Yasmeen was coming over at lunchtime to collect, at last, our fee for solving the case. We had invited Sofie to come, too.

At one o'clock we were all sitting around our kitchen table with glasses of milk and generous pieces of Grandma's pumpkin pie in front of us. Luau was camped out by his food bowl, chowing down on Cheesy Deans. I didn't even want to think what his breath was going to smell like later.

I couldn't wait to finally get my first taste of Grandma's pumpkin pie—at last. I had just picked up my fork to dig in when—*clink, clink, clink*—Dad tapped his milk glass with his knife. "While we are all here together, I just have a few words I want to say."

I couldn't believe it. Dad's Thanksgiving speech at a

time like this? Didn't he realize I'm a growing boy? It had been hours since my midmorning snack!

But Mom gave me one of her looks, and I laid my fork down. Dad laid on his glasses and fumbled in his shirt pocket. Nothing. He fumbled in his jeans pocket. Nothing. "It was here a minute ago," he said.

"Don't worry, Dad," I said. "Yasmeen, Sofie, Luau, and I will find it. But first, can we go ahead and eat?"

Dad smiled. "Dig in!"

We did. And just like I expected, Grandma's million-dollar pumpkin pie was delicious!

Grandma's Million-Dollar Pumpkin Pie

Be sure to ask an adult to help you prepare the pumpkin and use the oven.

3 eggs

2 cup mashed cooked pumpkin

¼ cup brown sugar

½ cup white sugar

¼ teaspoon salt

½ teaspoon each cinnamon, nutmeg

¾ teaspoon ginger

dash cloves

1 cup light cream

¼ cup mystery ingredient (read the book to get the clue!)

1 9-inch unbaked pie shell

Preheat oven to 350°F. In a large bowl, beat eggs. Add pumpkin, sugars, salt, and spices. Beat well. Gradually blend in cream. Pour into prepared shell and bake 65 minutes or until pie tests done.

Note: Pie pumpkins are smaller than the ones used for jack-o'-lanterns. You can find them in most grocery stores. To prepare a pumpkin, wash it thoroughly and bake it in a 350°F oven for about 45 minutes or until it can be pierced easily with a sharp knife. It's okay if the pumpkin collapses in on itself, but it doesn't have to. Remove it from the oven and let it cool. Then cut it in two, scrape out the seeds and strings, scoop the flesh from the skin, and mash it thoroughly or whiz it in a food processor. Seeds, string, and skin can be composted.

About the Author

Martha Freeman is known for her humorous novels for children and young adults, including *The Year My Parents Ruined My Life*, *The Trouble with Cats*, *Fourth Grade Weirdo*, and *The Trouble with Babies*. She is the author of three other Chickadee Court Mysteries featuring grade school detectives Alex and Yasmeen. *Kirkus Reviews* raved that *Who Is Stealing the 12 Days of Christmas?* was "breezy and humorous . . . guarantees laughs for every season." *Who Stole Halloween?* was a Texas Bluebonnet Award nominee, and *School Library Journal* called *Who Stole Uncle Sam?* "a funny, kid-friendly . . . fast-paced read." Ms. Freeman lives in Pennsylvania. Learn more on her website at www.marthafreeman.com.